It's a miracle Stacy has survived.
Too bad the killer
doesn't see it that way. . . .

There's a weird noise, like a yelp. It's coming from inside our house.

But a hand begins stroking my forehead. A deep voice says, "Go to sleep now, Stacy. Relax and sleep." I want to open my eyes, but I can't.

I run toward our back porch, and the screen door bangs open. Somebody runs out. He stares at me.

"Is she asleep?" Dad asks, and the voice murmurs, "Not yet."

This guy on the porch stares at me. I can't see his face, but I know he's staring. I feel it, the way words and ideas I need to know seem to sift through my skin and pour into my mind. He's scared. I know that too.

"Daddy, did they catch him?"

"Don't worry about that now," he says.

"But did they? I have to know!"

"No," he says. "They couldn't find out who it was. There were no witnesses."

It's harder and harder to speak. There's a humming in my head, and it moves Dad farther and farther away. I whisper, wondering if my whisper is real or only in my head. "I'm a witness. I saw him, Daddy."

THE
OTHER SIDE
OF DARK

Joan Lowery Nixon

Published by
Bantam Doubleday Dell Books for Young Readers
a division of
Bantam Doubleday Dell Publishing Group, Inc.
1540 Broadway
New York, New York 10036

The trademark Laurel-Leaf Library® is registered in the U.S. Patent and Trademark Office.

The trademark Dell® is registered in the U.S. Patent and Trademark Office.

ISBN: 0-440-96638-8

RL: 5.4

Reprinted by arrangement with Delacorte Press

Printed in the United States of America

One Previous Edition

May 1992

20

OPM

For Susan Cohen
with love

Chapter One

The dream is too long. It slithers and slips and gurgles deeply into midnight pools in which I see my own face looking back. It pounds with a scream that crashes into earth-torn caverns and is drowned; it surges with the babble of voices that splash against my ears; it whispers over words I can't understand.

I have cried out in my dream. I have called, and ages ago someone answered.

"Mom? Mama?"

My voice violently shakes the dream. I open my eyes, as with a trembling roar the dream rushes from my mind and my memory.

I'm in bed, but this is not my room. Across the room is a statue of a nurse. Her pencil is held in midair above her chart; her mouth is open enough that I can see some bubbles of saliva on her tongue; her eyes are stretched and glazed.

"Where's my mother?"

The statue comes to life. "Oh!" she says. "Oh, my, you're awake!" Fluttering like a moth between too many lights, she pats at my bed, jabs at the controls that rest on the nightstand, and trots to the door. "I'll be right back, Stacy," she says. She takes a step toward me with palms up as though she wanted to hold me where I am and repeats, "I will. I'll be back in a minute," then scrambles through the door.

"Where's my mother?" I call to the empty room. I try to sit up, but I can't. It makes me dizzy. My mouth is dry, and there's a spot on my left hip that is sore. What is happening to me? The blanket and sheet have slipped to one side, so I pull them up to my chest.

I gasp as my hands feel breasts that are rounded and firm. My shaking fingers slide past my waist, exploring, as the horror grows. I lift my head to look down, down at toes that lump the blanket near the foot of the bed, and the horror explodes in a scream. I am Stacy McAdams. I'm only thirteen years old, and I'm in the wrong body!

My room explodes with people, and they buzz like white-capped bees, reaching for my wrist, wrapping something around my left arm, and squeezing it until something beeps. And all the time I'm shouting, "Go away! I want my mother!"

A man with a trim blond beard sorts himself out from the confusion. He leans over me, studying me from under shaggy eyebrows, one hand gently stroking my forehead. "Stacy," he says, in a voice that pours like dark molasses, "I'm Dr. Peterson. I don't want to sedate you. I want to talk with you. Will you please stop shouting?"

I'm trembling so hard it feels as if the bed were shaking, and my voice is a raspy whimper. "Where's my mother? I need my mother. I'm afraid."

"Of course you are," he says, "but you don't need to be afraid. Everything will be all right." His hand keeps soothing my forehead, sopping up the fear until the trembling is gone and the bed is still.

The nurses have disappeared, except for a short, round one standing by the door. For some reason I notice that her blue eyes are surrounded by crinkly laugh lines, so I don't mind if she stays.

Dr. Peterson sits on the edge of my bed. My right hand disappears into his. "Now then," he says, "the members of your family are being contacted. They'll be here as soon as they can make it."

"My mother—"

But he hasn't finished. "You're in Houston's Braesforest Medical Center, under my care. You were brought here after hospital treatment for a gunshot wound."

I groan and screw up my face, trying to think, trying to remember.

"Relax," he says. "It doesn't matter now if you recall what happened. That can come later. The fact is that you've come out of what can best be called a semicomatose state, a type of coma."

"Dr. Peterson, listen to me!" I clutch both his hands, and my voice grates like a rusty gate. "There's something wrong. My body. It's not right. It's—"

"You were thirteen when you were brought here, Stacy. We've tried to keep you in a good state of health —as good as your condition would allow—so your body has grown and matured naturally."

"But I *am* thirteen!"

He shakes his head. "No, Stacy. You're seventeen."

"When my mother comes, she'll tell you that you're wrong!" I don't want to listen to what he has to say. I try to tell him to go away; but I can't talk and cry at the same time, and the tears get in my way.

He reaches to the table by my bed and hands me a fistful of tissues. They're soft, but they're heavy. My hands are heavy, my eyes are heavy, and the bed is a warm cocoon, shutting away the things I don't want to hear and see. Deliberately I slide into sleep.

This time I wake slowly, scrunching up my eyes, stretching and twisting and arching the way I love to do. "You wake up just the way Pansy does," my mother always says, as she shoos our lop-eared cat off the foot of my bed and tousles my hair. "Stacy, our other little cat."

"Stacy? You're awake?"

I open my eyes quickly at the sound of my father's voice. "Oh, Daddy, you're here! You're here! I need you!"

He quickly wraps me in a long hug. His chest, under his smooth white cotton shirt, smells cozy and warm, but my cheek grows wet from his tears. I hold him away, puzzled. "Daddy? I've never seen you cry."

There are hollows under his cheekbones, and his brown eyes seem strangely faded. His hair is thin on top. He's my father, but he isn't my father—at least not the way he was yesterday.

"Daddy, the doctor told me I've been here four years, that I'm not thirteen, I'm seventeen. It's not true, is it?" But as I study my father's face I know it has to be true, and I gasp, "How did it happen to me?"

"Nobody completely understands it. Not really.

You were shot, and the bullet did something to you that caused a kind of coma; but you didn't need life support. You were breathing on your own, and your vital signs were good. It's just that you were in a world of your own, and you couldn't or wouldn't leave it. The people here were able to help you sit in a chair and walk and even feed yourself if someone was with you. You have a physical therapist who has worked with you on exercises every day."

"I don't remember any of this."

He pats my hand. "I know, sweetheart. Mentally you weren't responding."

"Then why did I wake up?"

He shakes his head. "No one knows exactly. They can just guess. You fell and cut your hip. Then last week you developed an infection in the cut, and the doctors treated it with antibiotics and even some minor surgery. They think that maybe it was the reaction to the anesthetic that brought you out of the coma. I'm doing a bad job of telling you about it, I guess. Dr. Peterson can do a better job of explaining it to you than I can." My father wipes his cheeks with the back of one hand, then spots the box of tissues, wads one, and rubs it over his eyes.

The door opens, and a familiar face peers through. Donna's the original. I'm the carbon. "That beautiful dark hair, those tilted green eyes," Dad would say, and wink at Mom. "We've certainly got lovely daughters, Jeanne."

Donna shyly whispers, "Stacy?"

"Donna!" I hold out my arms to my sister, laughing

as she hurries through the door. She clumsily bumps against the end of the bed as she rushes to hug me.

"I like your hair that way," I mumble against her ear. "But don't ever scold me again about munching Twinkies. You're getting fat, big sister!"

She sits back and beams at me. Her tucked-in smile reminds me of so many times when she has been where I couldn't follow: her first dance; the red-haired basketball player she thought she was in love with when she was sixteen; the dorm friends she wrote about when she started college.

"I'm pregnant," she says. "In just two months you're going to be an aunt."

My mouth is open, and I know I'm making owl eyes, but I don't know what to say.

"Last year," she says, "Dennis and I were married." She glances at Dad from the corners of her eyes. "I had to promise that I'd get my degree, and I will—in May of next year. See, Dad, I'm keeping the promise."

"But I wasn't there!" I wail. "I was going to be your maid of honor. You always told me I could be."

She holds the palm of my hand up against her cheek. She's still smiling, but I see a terrible sorrow in her eyes. "Stacy, love, things were—well, so different. Dennis and I didn't have a big wedding. Just a few people and the priest."

"But you always said when you were married, you'd have a train six feet long! And loads of bridesmaids, all in blue, and wear the pearls that Grandma left to Mom."

Dad clears his throat as though he were about to say something, but Donna interrupts. "It doesn't matter," she says. She shakes her head, lays my hand gently on the blanket as though it were made of fine china, and awkwardly gets to her feet, one hand pressing the small of her back. "I can't wait till you meet Dennis. Dennis Kroskey. Hey, you'll have to get used to my new name!" She walks to the door, turning to say, "He's patiently biding time out in the hall because I wanted to see you first."

Dennis enters the room, and Donna props open the door. He's tall, with skin tanned the color of his reddish brown hair, and he has a summer smell of lots of soap and showers. I'll bet he plays tennis.

"I've met you before," he says, "when you were—sleeping."

"You came to see me?"

"Lots of times, with Donna. She introduced us, and she talked to you about our wedding, just in case you could hear her. Your family talked to you about everything that went on."

"Maybe that was part of my dream." There were so many voices, and they came and went for so long a time. I can't remember what they said. I don't want to remember. He's smiling, too, so I hurry to add, "Donna told me about the baby. I'm glad you're going to have a baby."

"So are we." He hugs Donna in such a special way that I ache right in the middle of my chest. I wasn't there when she fell in love and when she got married and when she first found out she was going to have a baby. I have to get used to all this at once, and it makes me feel lonely and shut out, no matter what they tell me.

I take a long breath, trying to keep things going right. "I'll baby-sit for you whenever you want. I guess I should say I'll baby-sit if Mom gives me a chance. She'll be so crazy about that baby the rest of us might not get to hold it until it's old enough to go to school."

No one laughs. No one answers. There's a funny kind of chill, like when you open the freezer door on a hot day and the icy air spills over your feet. "When's Mom coming?" My words plop into the cold. "Where is Mom?"

Dr. Peterson is suddenly there, head forward, his shaggy eyebrows leading the way like the prow of a ship. "Donna and Dennis," he says, "we'll keep your visit short. Why don't you come back to see Stacy tomorrow?"

Donna quickly kisses me, Dennis pats my feet, and they disappear before I can protest. The door swings shut, and the room is silent.

Dr. Peterson lifts my wrist in strong fingers and looks at his watch.

I try to tug my arm away from him. "You interrupted," I tell him. "I was asking a question, and I want an answer!"

"Take this," he orders. He hands me a pill and a glass of water from the table.

"Not now."

"Yes, now."

As I obey, quickly gulping the pill, he nods at my father, and Dad leans forward, holding my hand again. His skin is clammy and hot, and he has to clear his throat a couple of times before he can talk.

"Honey," he says, "all along we've had faith in you.

We knew you wouldn't give up. Remember even when you were just a little girl and you'd be so independent and set on getting your own way? You've always had a lot of courage, Stacy, and—"

"Daddy, tell me now. Where's Mom?"

He is hurting, and I can't help him. I don't even want to help him. My toes and fingers are warm and relaxed, and a numb feeling is seeping through me. It's like the drowsy waking-sleeping in the early morning after the alarm has been turned off. But I'm awake, and I hear what he's saying.

"The day you were shot—" His words are jagged pebbles on a dry, dusty road, and his voice trips as he stumbles through them. "Your mother was shot too. But Jeanne—oh, Stacy, Jeanne was killed."

"No," I answer, because I don't believe these strange words that are as hollow as shouts inside a tunnel, ringing and echoing and sliding away. My father is gray and crumpled, and he's crying. I try to pat his hand with fingers that are too heavy to lift. Something is wrong. Maybe it's still part of the dream, and I'll wake up and tell Mom about this crazy dream while we're making breakfast, and she'll give me a little swat on my backside and say, "For goodness' sake, stop talking and eat, or you're going to be late for school."

"Tell me everything that happened," I murmur, wanting the dream to be complete. "No one has told me."

It takes a few minutes for my father to answer. His voice seems farther away, but I clearly hear every word. "Donna said you were going to the backyard to sunbathe," he begins.

I remember. I was wearing my new red shorts, and I had Pansy with me. There wasn't any smog, and it was a golden day, and I wanted a head start on my tan.

"We don't know what happened next," he says. "Donna went to the grocery store down at the boulevard to get a couple of things. She came home and found that the front door was unlocked. Your mother was lying in the den. Donna said she screamed at Jeanne to get up, but she didn't move. Donna telephoned for an ambulance, and then she remembered you. She ran outside and found you lying on the grass near the back porch steps."

I hear the words, but I don't feel them. I am in a tunnel, but I can still hear what Dad says. Except that his words get mixed up with the other sounds and voices that are in my head.

There's a weird noise, like a yelp. It's coming from inside our house.

But a hand begins stroking my forehead. A deep voice says, "Go to sleep now, Stacy. Relax and sleep." I want to open my eyes, but I can't.

I run toward our back porch, and the screen door bangs open. Somebody runs out. He stares at me.

"Is she asleep?" Dad asks, and the voice murmurs, "Not yet."

This guy on the porch stares at me. I can't see his face, but I know he's staring. I feel it, the way words and ideas I need to know seem to sift through my skin and pour into my mind. He's scared. I know that too.

"Daddy, did they catch him?"

"Don't worry about that now," he says.

"But did they? I have to know!"

"No," he says. "They couldn't find out who it was. There were no witnesses."

It's harder and harder to speak. There's a humming in my head, and it moves Dad farther and farther away. I whisper, wondering if my whisper is real or only in my head. "I'm a witness. I saw him, Daddy."

"Hush, Stacy," Daddy says. "Don't try to talk now. Go to sleep."

The sounds in my mind melt together and dissolve the words. I am so tired. I don't ever remember having a dream in which I felt tired. I wonder what my mother will tell me about this dream.

Chapter Two

When morning comes, gray light poking around the edges of the venetian blinds, I wake and know this has not been a dream. As though a tape recorder were inside my brain, part of last night's conversation comes through loud and clear.

A picture appears. I am standing in our backyard. I'm listening, wondering what it was I heard. "Mom?" I call as I walk toward the porch steps. "Are you all right?"

But the door suddenly slams open, hitting the siding on the house with a clatter, and someone races out. He pauses on the second step as we stare at each other. But I can't see his face!

"Show me your face," I say aloud. "You're someone I know. I remember that much!"

The face is blank. But there's something in his hand. It's a gun. He points it at me. I can't move. I can't make a sound. I want to cry out, "Mom!"

Mom.

Some part of my mind has clutched and hidden what Dad told me about Mom; but now his words spill out, and I have to face them. I roll onto my stomach and cry, the pillow stuffed against my mouth. I cry until no more tears will come, and dry, hiccuping shudders shake my body. The soggy pillow smells sour, so I push it to the floor. I'll never see my mother again.

The door snaps open, and a tall, angular nurse, who matches the crispness of her uniform, strides to my bed. "Well, hi," she says. "I'm Alice." I can tell that she's taking in the pillow on the floor and my swollen eyes, but she doesn't react until all the temperature-pulse business has been accomplished. She checks under the bandage on my hip, makes a note on her chart, puts it down, and for the first time looks at me as though I were a person. "How about a shower before breakfast?" she asks. "It will help you feel a lot better."

"Yesterday I got kind of dizzy when I tried to sit up."

"That was yesterday, and that was the medication."

"Have I got out of bed to take showers before?"

She smiles. "Every day, and I'm usually the one who's given them to you."

My face is hot. I'm embarrassed that I blushed, but she doesn't seem to notice. The shower does make me feel better on the outside. I hold my face up to the water, feeling its sting on my forehead and scalp.

But nothing has helped on the inside. Maybe I can't be helped, because a hollow has been carved in there, and inside that hollow there are no feelings at all.

Alice, making sure I'm steady on my feet, leaves me to towel-dry my hair. She hums under her breath as she makes my bed.

There's a small mirror over the sink in my bathroom. I drop the towel and study myself in the mirror. It's the weirdest sensation. I feel that I'm looking at Donna the way Donna looked when I was thirteen. The person in that mirror is different from the one I was used to seeing. The face is thinner with shadows under the cheekbones. I remember when my best friend, Jan, and I would stick our faces toward the mirror and suck in our cheeks and say, "This is what we'll look like when we grow up and are beautiful!"

I wonder how the eyes in the mirror can droop with so much pain when I feel absolutely empty inside.

Alice brings me a short gown sprigged with blue violets. "The nurses thought you'd like something pretty," she says, adding, "Norma picked it out."

I don't know what to say. I think I mumble, "Thank you."

She glances at me from the corners of her eyes. The shyness doesn't match her efficient look. "We're all so glad that you recovered. We really care about our patients, especially the young ones. Especially you, Stacy. You've got most of your life ahead of you, and we—" She stops, and the briskness takes over. "Your sister's going to bring some of her clothes for you."

"Don't I have any clothes here? What did I wear?"

"During the day we put you into cotton knit jumpsuits, which you could wear when the therapist helped you ride the exercise bike and use the other equipment." She reaches into the small closet, pulls out a shapeless gray thing, and holds it up, its arms and legs dangling. It looks like an ad showing what happens when you use the wrong brand of soap.

All I can say is "Yeech!"

She laughs and tucks me between the stiff sheets, cranks my bed until I'm sitting upright, and hands me a hairbrush so that I can brush my hair.

Breakfast is brought in, and while I'm munching through the eggs' curly brown edges, a girl appears in the open doorway.

She looks at me as though she were afraid of me, and for a moment I don't know who she is.

"Stacy," she says, still in the doorway, "I'm Jan. Can I come in?"

"Jan?" I know I'm sitting there with my mouth open, but it's hard to believe that this tall auburn-haired girl in the pink, tailored shirt and tight jeans and makeup that looks like a cosmetic ad is my friend Jan Briley.

Her knees seem a little stiff—or maybe it's the jeans. She shoves a small package toward me, backs off, and perches on the edge of the armchair across from the bed. "It's not much," she says. "Just some lipstick and eye shadow and mascara and stuff I thought you'd need."

"Thanks." This isn't Jan. It can't be Jan. I shiver and push the breakfast tray away.

"You look—you look good, Stacy. How do you feel?"

"Okay."

"You'll feel lots better when your makeup's on and you've done something with your hair. Do you have hot rollers?" She looks embarrassed. Her fingers are white from gripping the arms of the chair. "Of course you wouldn't have them here. I should have brought mine, I guess."

"It's okay." I look at her hair closely. "You never used to wear your hair like that. You used to wad it up in those big brown barrettes to keep it out of your eyes when we played baseball. Do you still play on the team?"

"Team? Oh, no." She gives a funny little laugh and says, "There's a mirror in the package. Why not get it out?"

"What for?"

"So you can put on your makeup."

"Mom lets me—let me wear lipstick, but I don't know what to do with the eye stuff."

"Oh. I didn't think about that. I just take makeup for granted, like brushing my teeth or wearing shoes."

"How long have you worn real makeup?"

"Well gosh, Stacy, for ages. After all, I'm seventeen." She pauses. "And so are you."

I shake my head. "I've got to get used to that. I still feel like I'm thirteen. I feel like everything took place yesterday."

"I'm sorry about what happened—all of it. When they took you to the hospital and thought you might die, I wanted to die too. I couldn't bear to lose you. And then last night your father called me, and I couldn't believe it. I just sat right down on the floor and cried and cried, I was so glad you were going to be all right again." Jan leans forward, forearms resting on her knees. "Do you want to talk about it?"

I can't help it, but I feel as though she were one of Donna's friends, not mine. It's hard to answer. "I haven't remembered all of it yet."

"Oh," she says, and looks relieved. I don't know

what I expected. Sympathy? Maybe even curiosity. This Jan doesn't want to know what I could tell her.

I have no idea what to say to her. I guess, from the way she starts squirming as though the chair had lumps in it, that she feels the same way. This is my best friend, Jan, to whom I told even my secret thoughts, and now I'm blank.

But I make a desperate stab. "What are things like at school?"

Jan sits upright, looking thankful, as though she'd just passed a math test she hadn't studied for. "Oh, same old grind. Suzie—you remember Suzie Lindly—anyhow, poor Suzie got married last week to a guy who is really out of it. I mean totally out. Only everybody knows she had to."

"Why did she have to?"

Jan blinks a couple of times, her mouth open. "Honestly, Stacy. You know. Because she's pregnant."

"Oh." I feel myself blushing again, and I'm mad at myself for being so dumb, for being a little kid.

Jan takes a deep breath and picks up speed, like a train making up time after almost getting derailed. "And Bick is quarterback and is the big thing in the sports section of the newspaper each weekend and has a ton of colleges wanting him next year."

"Bick—that skinny guy in ninth grade?"

Jan rolls her eyes. "He's no longer skinny, needless to say, and he's a senior and really something to look at. I dated him a couple of times." She smiles, and I can see that she's waiting for me to be impressed.

But I giggle. "I'm sorry, Jan. All I can see in my mind is gawky, skinny Bick who likes to make those awful loud burps while we're eating lunch. Remember, he sent you a note in study hall one day and got yelled at by Mr. Hadley, and you said you'd rather drop dead than have anything to do with Bick?"

There's a long pause. Finally her voice comes out as tight as a stretched rubber band. "I'd forgotten. That was such a long time ago."

We stare at each other for a few moments until I stammer, "I guess it was." Desperately I blurt out, "Well, tell me about yourself."

"Sure. B.J. talked me into joining the camera club. You remember B.J., don't you?"

"The quiet girl with the blond braids."

Jan laughs. "No more braids, and B.J. really blossomed. We're all jealous. Anyhow, I went into photography in a big way and got some black-and-whites and one color shot accepted for the yearbook last year. So I'm on the staff this year, and B.J. and I are saving our money for a camera trip in Yellowstone Park in July. B.J. says—"

"Sounds like B.J.'s a good friend."

"My best. She's so much fun, and—" Jan stops. "Of course, you've always been my best friend, too, Stacy, and when you get back to school—"

We just look at each other. I don't feel jealous because this Jan is another person in another world. This isn't my comfortable, forever-and-ever best friend, Jan. Besides, the hollow place is still inside me. I can't feel anything at all.

Jan jumps to her feet. "I've got to leave pretty soon. Let me get some makeup on you first."

I'm still clutching the package. "You don't have to."

"I want to. Really. You can use the little hand mirror to watch."

She has taken the package out of my hands and tears it open, so I don't object. I just let her smear on creams and oils and all sorts of stuff, obeying directions as she tells me to close my eyes, open my eyes, and hold my mouth just right so she can add the lipstick. She gives me instructions as she goes, but it's hard for me to pay attention. I keep thinking about the Friday nights when she'd stay over at my house or I would at hers, and we'd put on our pajamas and sit on the bed eating cookies and cheese puffs and all sorts of junk while we watched TV and rolled each other's hair. I wish she'd go away.

Finally she steps back, stares at me and gasps, "Stacy, you're really beautiful! Look in the mirror. Look at yourself."

Dr. Peterson comes into the room, stands at the foot of the bed, and studies me so appreciatively that I don't have to look into the mirror.

"Seventeen, going on twenty-six," he says. He's not talking to me. It's to someone else who's sitting here, someone I don't even know.

I introduce him to Jan, who beams at him like a beauty contestant meeting the judge, grabs for her handbag, and says, "I know you're busy, and I'll get out of your way."

"Stick around if you like," he says.

But Jan squeezes my hand and rolls her eyes upward in a way I remember, meaning, "Isn't he gorgeous?" and backs through the door, saying to me, "I'll see you tomorrow."

I can't help giggling, but it surprises me by sounding like a sob.

"Don't cry," Dr. Peterson says. "One thing I learned when I was married is that crying does ugly, smeary things to a woman's mascara."

"I don't know anything about mascara."

"Well, you've got plenty of it on."

For the first time I look into the little mirror and feel even more alienated than before from the body I'm in.

"Want to wash your face? I can wait."

"Yes." I start to climb out of bed, then change my mind. I kind of like the way that girl in the mirror looks. Maybe I can save it for just a little while. Maybe I could get used to looking like that. "Never mind," I murmur. I tuck the blanket around my hips and sneak another look in the mirror.

He sits on the side of the bed. "Do you want to talk to me?"

"About what?"

"About what you remember."

I know I'm scowling, screwing up the muscles in my face until they hurt, trying, trying, trying so hard to think. "I don't remember enough."

"Don't work at it so hard. It will all come back to you."

"What if it doesn't?"

"I think it will. You said you saw him—the guy who shot you."

"I didn't think that you heard me."

He doesn't answer, just shifts his weight, making the bed wobble, and waits for me to go on.

I hug my knees against my chest. "I can't see his face, but I know his name. It's somewhere in my head!"

"Take it easy. One thing at a time."

"If I could just remember, I could tell the police. I could identify him. What if he gets away?"

"It's been four years already since the crime took place. A little more time won't matter. Why don't you talk to me about the way you feel? You've had to make a lot of mental adjustments in the past few hours."

"I don't want to talk about anything."

"I'd like to talk about your mother."

"No!" I sound so angry I'm surprised, because I don't feel angry. I don't feel anything. I'm a robot with nothing inside but gears that make me move and talk. I try to soften my voice and add, "I can't. Not yet anyway."

"Okay," Dr. Peterson says. "I'll be here when you want me."

My breath comes out in a long shudder. "I want to go home."

He smiles. He has a nice smile. It melts across his face, matching the deep syrup of his voice. "Pretty soon," he says. "We just have to make sure you're over the infection and the anesthetic and all that stuff."

In spite of the way I feel, I can't help reacting. "Doctors don't say things like 'all that stuff.'"

"Oh? What do doctors say?"

"You know. All sorts of professional things that nobody can understand."

He stands up, pats my hand, and moves toward the

door. "Okay. There must be a medical book around here someplace. I'll look through it and find something that sounds good."

The door plops shut behind him, and the room settles into stillness. I remember in Grandma's house how she'd go through the living room and dining room every evening, pulling down the window shades against the dusk, one by one shutting out the night, shielding the house, enclosing it in a white-fringed safety. My mind is doing the same thing. I know that thoughts should be racing through my mind, tumbling over each other. I should be rolling in memories, wading through pain to all the new things I've seen and heard. But bit by bit my mind is shutting itself in, shielding itself from everything but one thought: *Who was the person I saw on our back stairs?*

It's his turn to die.

Chapter Three

A reporter comes to my room.

But Donna arrived first with a suitcase filled with blouses and jeans and underwear and a pair of brown sandals, so I'm sitting in a chair, dressed in jeans that are too loose and short and a T-shirt that's definitely too snug and sandals that actually fit.

"I had to guess on sizes," Donna said as she tugged at the belt that keeps the jeans from falling around my hips. "I didn't realize that you'd grown so tall and that you're so slender. I guess I keep thinking of you the way you were when you were thirteen."

"That makes two of us," I answered. I wish Donna hadn't helped me get dressed. I felt the same way I did last year—no, the year I was twelve—and took swimming lessons and all the girls had to change clothes together in the dressing room. Some of them were starting to grow breasts, and I'd sneak little looks while I was trying to keep my own chest covered, feeling miserable, hoping no one was looking at me.

I know, Donna's my sister. But in a way she isn't my sister. She's a grown woman, with a baby growing in-

side her, and it makes her so different I really don't
know her at all.

There's a quick knock at the door, and it opens
before either Donna or I can answer. A woman steps in
and takes in Donna and me and everything around us
with a glance that sweeps the room like a vacuum
cleaner.

Seemingly satisfied, she looks directly at me. "Hi!"
she says, and her grin is broad and full of teeth. She's
skinny, with frizzy blond hair that sticks out in every
direction. Loose strands straggle over her eyes and fly
away from her forehead. Straps for her handbag and
camera case are tangled on her left shoulder.

For a moment Donna and I just stare at her, so she
quickly adds, "Didn't they tell you I was coming? I'm
Brandi Mayer, a reporter from the *Houston Evening
News.*" She peers at me. "You're Stacy McAdams?"

I watch a strand of hair flop across her glasses.
They're huge and round and too big for her. She pushes
her glasses up on her nose but doesn't seem to notice
the hair in her eyes. "Yes. I'm Stacy," I answer.

Donna steps slightly in front of me, taking charge.
"I'm Stacy's sister, Donna Kroskey. Maybe I'd better
call the clinic's supervisor. No one here told us a reporter was coming. I really don't know if you should be
here or not."

Brandi pushes up her glasses again and perches on
the edge of my bed, since I'm in the only chair. "Com-
munication foul-ups," she says. "Happens all the time.
Drives me absolutely batty." She pulls a tiny tape recorder out of her handbag. The strand of hair drifts

back over her forehead. "You mind if I tape this?" she asks.

"Tape what?"

Brandi says, "If you don't know, I'd better fill you in. I'm doing a story for the *News* about Stacy. My editor is real soft on human-interest stuff, and he thinks that what happened to Stacy, coming out of a coma and all that, ought to make a good feature story."

"But how did he know about Stacy?" Donna asks.

"Easy," Brandi says. "Medical news is a regular beat. We check the hospitals and clinics all the time, and we have people who call us about things they think might make stories." She smiles at me. "Okay. Now that you know what I'm doing here, do you want to talk?"

Donna answers. "Not yet. I'm going to call the supervisor's office and make sure this is all right. But first, we're going to ask Stacy if she wants this interview."

I shrug. "I don't care." A puff of hair drifts over Brandi's glasses again. She probably doesn't know what a mess her hair is. It looks as if she were caught in the rain and then in the wind. So I say, "Look, before you ask me any questions, do you want to comb your hair? You can use my bathroom mirror."

"Stacy," Donna mumbles. She looks embarrassed.

Brandi just gets up, goes into the bathroom, and comes right back. "Looks the way it's supposed to look," she says. "I worked hard to get it like this."

"I can't get mine to do that," Donna says. "I think it's the wrong length."

"You're kidding," I tell them. "You mean it's supposed to look messy?"

"Stacy! You're being rude."

But Brandi grins. "It's the latest thing, kid. But you wouldn't know that. You're still into what was going on four years ago. That's great! Real reader-interest stuff. How do you feel about the new cars and new movies and—"

"Wait!" Donna says, so while Donna telephones we sit and stare at each other. Brandi impatiently fiddles with her tape recorder.

Donna hangs up the receiver and says, "The woman in the supervisor's office says it's all right, but maybe I should try to get in touch with Dad and see what he thinks."

"Could I just take a couple of pictures and get some basic answers from Stacy while you're doing that?" Brandi looks at her watch. "I've got another appointment in less than an hour, and it's over near the Loop."

"It's all right with me," I tell them, so while Donna makes the call Brandi quickly aims her camera at me and snaps a few pictures. Then she tucks away the camera, turns on her tape recorder, wiggles into a shoulders-back alertness, and says, "Stacy McAdams—and that's spelled M-C and not M-A-C. Right?"

"Dad's not in his office right now," Donna says. She comes to stand beside me and rests a hand on my shoulder.

"If I ask anything you object to, just stop me," Brandi says. And without waiting for Donna to answer, she asks me, "What did it feel like, Stacy, coming back to the real world after four years asleep?"

The question throws me. "I—I don't exactly know yet. There's a lot to get used to."

"New songs, new fashions, new television shows," Brandi says. "Sleeping Beauty, coming back to the world. Hmmm. That's good."

"No. That's wrong. Sleeping Beauty slept for a hundred years, and everyone else slept with her. Everything would be the same when she woke up."

"Details, details. Doesn't matter," Brandi says. "What did you remember when you woke up?"

I close my eyes for a moment, thinking, trying so hard to think. I can see our screen door flying open. I can see the guy with the gun running out and pausing as he sees me standing there. And I can see him raise the gun, pointing it at me. But I can't see his face!

"She's getting tired." Donna breaks in.

"No. I'm trying to see his face, and I can't!"

"Whose face?" Brandi asks.

"The guy who shot Mom. He ran out our back door. The screen door slammed open. I was standing there. We looked at each other, and he raised the gun. He shot me. I know him. I know his name. I think that's why he shot me."

Brandi leans toward me eagerly. "You're an eyewitness! You saw your mother's murderer!"

"Yes."

"So tell me about him."

"I can't remember his face."

"But you said that you know him."

"I do!"

"Do you remember his name?"

I scrunch up my face. Trying to remember hurts. It aches. "It's in my head. It's like I can touch it. But it won't come close enough."

Brandi's eyes sparkle. "Think hard. Maybe all of a sudden it will all come back to you."

Donna interrupts. "I don't think we should even talk about it. Maybe it would be traumatic for Stacy to remember. We ought to leave it up to Dr. Peterson. Stacy is all that's important. The rest isn't."

I speak up. "It's important to me to know who that guy is. He killed my mother!"

Donna's arms are around me. "Shush, shush. It's okay, Stacy. Don't get upset."

"I hate him, Donna!"

"And you want to see him get what he deserves!" Brandi's eyes are bright.

"Yes!" The hollow inside me begins to fill, churning upward with boiling bubbles of anger, until there is nothing inside me but a burning red hatred for the man I saw, the killer, the murderer, the person who took my mother away from me.

Donna's cheek is against mine. She's holding me tightly. "Stop!" she says to Brandi. "Please stop and get out of here. This isn't good for Stacy."

"Listen to her. She wants to remember."

"Go away!" Donna stands and takes a step toward Brandi.

"Okay," Brandi says. She climbs off the bed and smiles at Donna as though they were best friends. "I'm going. I'm gone." She fishes a business card from her pocket and hands it to me. "Thanks for the interview, Stacy. If you remember anything else about this guy who shot you, please give me a call. Okay?"

I just nod and stuff the card into the pocket of my jeans.

Donna follows Brandi into the hall, and in a couple of minutes she comes back with Alice.

"Got a little excited, did we?" Alice asks. Before I can answer, she wraps a cuff around my left arm and takes my blood pressure. She beams at Donna and at me. "Very good. Nice and normal. No harm done."

"I still don't think they should—"

"The supervisor has a new secretary. She didn't know—"

"Patients should have privacy, and—"

"I agree. I agree. Unfortunately they don't let nurses make the rules, although—"

I get to my feet, and the walls of the room lean a little to the left and then to the right. So I rest my head against the wall to steady it.

"Oh, Stacy," Donna says, and her arms are around me. I can feel the warm bulge of her belly against mine.

"Donna," I murmur against her hair, "I want to go home. Take me home."

"As soon as the doctor says so."

"Where is he?"

Alice gently pulls me away from Donna, leads me to the bed, and pats me into place. "Mrs. Montez is your physical therapist, Stacy. She'll be in soon. She wants to talk to you. Just be patient, honey. You'll be home in no time." Task accomplished, Alice rustles from the room.

I close my eyelids. The anger glows against them. "I wish I could see his face."

Donna leans over to kiss my forehead. She gives a little grunt as she bends, and I'm very much aware of the baby who is making her body so thick in the middle that it's hard for her to lean over the bed.

"I'm going to let you rest now," Donna says. "I have to get to class. I'll see you later."

Her face is close to mine, and I can see the tiny beads of perspiration that lie on her upper lip like a glistening mustache. "Donna," I say, grabbing her right hand and holding it tightly, "do you remember a couple of years ago when Mom was pregnant?"

"That was more than a couple of years ago, Stacy. You were only ten."

I groan. "Ten—whenever. Oh, Donna, I was so excited about Mom's baby, and I'd rest my hand on her stomach and feel it kick. And when she lost it, it hurt so much it nearly killed me."

There are tears on Donna's cheeks. "I know. It hurt all of us."

I struggle to sit up and wrap my arms around her. "I didn't mean to make you cry. I'm so mixed up. I mean, I think about Mom having a baby, but not you. And now that you're grown-up and pregnant I can't get used to it. It's like you should be Mom and not Donna, and it makes me feel strange and faraway and—oh, Donna, I don't even know how to tell you what's in my head."

But Donna soothes me, patting my back and nuzzling her cheek against mine. "It's okay, Stacy. It's okay. Calm down. Everything's not going to happen at once. It's going to take awhile for you to get things straight. Don't punish yourself by trying to rush it. Just relax. Just take each day as it comes."

We hold each other without talking. The room is warm. The window spills sunlight onto the beige tile floor, and the voices in the hall hum in the background like contented bees. Donna is the big sister, the comforting one, yet the hurt we share is the same, and it flows between us. I can feel how much Donna misses Mom too. I begin to realize that there'd be questions she'd want to ask Mom, little scary sparks that Mom could pat out with a smile and a few words. There'd be the baby clothes to buy together, the excitement to share about the first grandchild.

As I close my eyes I see our screen door fly open. Someone runs out and pauses on the steps. He stares at me. He raises the gun and points it at me. But where is his face? For Donna, for me, I must see his face!

Donna leans back, holding my shoulders. "Are you all right now, Stacy?"

I nod. The storm blew away some of the clutter in my mind, and I found my sister. "Thanks, Donna."

"Whenever you need me, I'll be here," she says.

I pat her stomach and smile and answer, "Whenever *you* need *me.* I'll be here too."

Alice opens the door in a hurry, nimbly stepping back, saying, "Stacy, this is Mrs. Montez."

The physical therapist bursts past her into my room, leaning forward a little, breaking a path with her chin and the end of her nose. She's short and solid with clipped gray hair, and she's packed into a rose velour jogging suit. She checks the chart at the end of my bed, grins at it and then at me.

"All that good, regular exercise has paid off," she says. "Aren't we proud of ourselves!"

"I don't remember exercising," I tell her. "And I'm sorry, but I don't even remember you."

Her left hand chops at the air, as though she were cutting off something unnecessary. "Doesn't matter if you remember or not," she says. "What matters is that I kept you in good physical shape. Once you're over the temporary effects of your operation, you'll find yourself in fine condition, thanks to my care and skill."

Behind Mrs. Montez's back Alice winks at me.

"You may think this all sounds immodest," Mrs. Montez says, half turning to include Alice, who blinks and looks embarrassed, "but the body is like a machine that must stay fine-tuned in order to operate correctly. And keeping you in condition was my job." She beams again, looking so pleased with herself she reminds me of the Cheshire cat in *Alice in Wonderland.*

"So," she says, bouncing a little on her toes, "if Dr. Peterson allows it, tomorrow morning I'll put you through your paces. Then, after you return to your home, you can keep up the good work. Do you have a swimming pool?"

"No."

"Exercise cycle?"

"I don't think so."

"Rowing machine? Oh, never mind. Of course, you don't have any of the things you'll need. No one ever does. Well, I'll just trot off and see what we can do about it."

Without another word she charges from the room. Alice smiles sheepishly and whispers to me, "She's really awfully good. One of the best."

A white-coated orderly with shaggy yellow hair comes in with a lunch tray. His gap-toothed grin is friendly as he arranges the tray on the table by my bed and swings it around in front of me.

"Thanks, Monty," Alice says.

"No problem," Monty says, and dashes off before Alice can hoist me up and plump up my pillows.

There's nothing special on the tray, but I'm hungry. I don't pay much attention to what I'm eating. I'm tired, and after I've finished my lunch, I push the table away, lie back, and go to sleep.

The dreams don't make sense as they lap one into another, trailing through the afternoon. I wake to long shadows in a room lit with late orange sunlight.

The light touches Donna in her chair, brushing brightness into her hair and on her cheek. Her head is bent as she reads a newspaper, and a little worry wrinkle flickers on her forehead.

I stretch lazily, arching my back, and Donna looks up.

"You're purring," she said. "I remember how Mom said you were like a little cat the way you stretched. You always used to purr."

"I must have slept a long time."

Donna sighs and hands me the newspaper. "I wish I hadn't let that reporter interview you."

I wiggle up, sitting cross-legged, the newspaper on my lap. There, on the front page, are two photographs of me—one my class picture when I was thirteen and in the seventh grade and the other the picture Brandi took this morning. Two girls, so very different, yet they're both me. One I recognize, but the other is someone I don't even know. I keep staring at the photos until Donna says, in the same tone of voice she'd use if she'd found a roach in the bathtub, "She even used that 'Sleeping Beauty' stuff."

For the first time I read the headline over the pictures and story: SLEEPING BEAUTY AWAKES TO NEW WORLD. "Does she write what I said about her messy hair?" I ask Donna.

Donna groans. "Read it."

So I do. Brandi's story is not too bad, just a little dramatic, and she did put in the part about her hair, only she didn't use the word *messy*. She made everything seem more exciting than it was, especially the part about how I was the only one who could identify my mother's murderer.

I throw the newspaper on the bed and complain to Donna, "She didn't write things the way they happened. She makes it sound like any minute now I'm going to remember who I saw. But I can't! I want to, and I'm trying, but I still can't!"

"It's my fault that story was written," Donna says. "I should have sent her away."

"Don't blame yourself. It's not your fault." I sneak another look at the girls in the photographs. "I wonder where she got my seventh-grade picture."

"Not from Dad or from me," Donna says. "She might have got it from your school or from one of your friends."

"Maybe Jan." I study the picture the reporter took. Am I really as grown-up as I look in that second picture? Donna sighs and mumbles something else about making a mistake, so I quickly say, "It doesn't matter. It's just a dumb story. I bet nobody will even read it."

"Of course, they'll read it!" Donna says. "And what worries me is what if—"

I wait a moment, watching worry pucker her forehead and turn down the corners of her lips. When she doesn't finish what she was saying I ask, "What if what?"

"Nothing," Donna says.

"You were going to say something. Don't just stop like that. I want to know what's bothering you."

Donna tries to smile. "Stacy, my thoughts were just wandering around. I don't even remember what I had in mind."

"But—"

She stands up and hugs me. "I've got to get home and put something together for dinner. Dennis made dinner the last three nights, and I promised I'd take my turn tonight. He comes home starving to death, and I need to stop by the grocery store and get lettuce because we're out . . ."

Donna is talking nonstop, not letting me get in another word. I remember that technique of hers, and I have to smile. Okay. She doesn't have to tell me now what she has in mind. She'll come out with it sooner or later.

"Dad will be here to see you tonight," she says as she reaches the door. "And I'll be back tomorrow morning. Bye, Stacy." The door closes before I have a chance to answer.

I turn on the bedside lamp, take another quick look at the photographs, and go to the bathroom mirror. As I comb my hair I study my face. This is me, Stacy McAdams, and I have to start getting used to it. This is how other people see me. This is how people who read the newspaper will see me. This is how—

I suck in a deep breath and hang onto the edge of the basin as what Donna meant suddenly socks me. Brandi wrote that I could identify the murderer. What if the killer reads that? What will he do?

"Somebody help me!" I whisper to the girl in the mirror. "I've got to be able to see his face!"

Chapter Four

The bones in my legs are like Jell-O, and chills shiver up and down my spine. Somehow I make it back to the chair and drop into it, trying to think, wondering what I can do.

A voice makes me jump. "That Sleeping Beauty stuff was cornball."

"Dr. Peterson! I didn't hear you come in."

"Obviously. What makes you so jumpy? Did you think I was another reporter?"

"No. I just had a lot on my mind. I—" I look right into his eyes. "I was scared. I *am* scared."

He sits on the bed and rests his elbows on his legs, leaning toward me. "I didn't know that reporter had been allowed to visit you," he says. "We have someone new on the front desk, and she didn't understand the situation. I'm sorry it happened. No one else from the media will be allowed to see you while you're here."

"It's not your fault."

"Your sister chewed us all out." He smiles.

"What if the guy who murdered my mother reads that story? It says I'm an eyewitness."

He nods. "He may not read it. That was four years

ago. He may be thousands of miles away from here. He might even be in jail somewhere. Or dead."

"What if he isn't?"

He shrugs and looks as though he wished he had an answer. "Don't worry about him," he manages to say.

Don't worry? Oh, sure. I grip the arms of the chair. But the telephone rings. Someone at the front desk tells Dr. Peterson that two detectives from the Houston Police Department have arrived, that they want to talk to me.

Dr. Peterson opens the door wide and leans against the wall, arms folded, waiting for the detectives to join us.

"You don't have to stay," I tell him.

"I don't have anything important to do," he answers. "A head transplant, but that can wait."

"I don't need a baby-sitter."

"Doctors never baby-sit. Their fees are too high."

"I'm not going to laugh at your jokes. It will only encourage you."

Two tall men block the door for a moment. Smoothly one steps aside, then follows the other into my room. They look the way I'd imagine detectives should look. Their business suits are taut across their broad shoulders, and they're both big men. They have brown hair, and one has a mustache. It's their eyes, I think, that label them as detectives. It doesn't matter that the mustached one has brown eyes and the other has blue. I know they really see me, every detail of me, and they're trying to probe below the surface, poking at the doors to my mind.

Markowitz and Johns, they tell me and shake hands

with Dr. Peterson. Markowitz has the mustache. I'll try to remember that.

A voice comes from the doorway, and Dad appears. "What is this? Stacy, are you all right?"

Dr. Peterson fills Dad in, and everyone goes through the introduction thing again.

Dad shakes his head. "I don't think Stacy is up to this yet." But his words come out in a question, and he's looking at Dr. Peterson, not at me.

"Stacy can handle it," Dr. Peterson says.

"Hey, look at me, Daddy. I'm dressed and out of bed. I'm feeling a lot better. Honest!" I stand up and give Dad a hug.

He hugs me tightly, awkwardly. The shock I feel takes away the comfort I used to feel in my father's hugs. My head once fitted snugly against his chest, and now I find myself looking over his shoulder. We stand back and stare at each other.

"You might want to sit down, Stacy," Detective Johns says to me. "We won't be long. Just a few questions." He shoves his hands in his pockets, then takes them out again. He doesn't seem to know what to do with his hands. I bet he's trying to stop smoking.

"It's about that newspaper article, isn't it?" Dad asks as I move away from him and sit in the only chair. Everyone else is standing, and it makes me feel kind of strange.

"Yes," Detective Markowitz says. "Stacy, according to the interview you gave the reporter for the *Evening News,* you saw a person run out of your house, the person who shot you."

I nod. "But—"

"It's been four years," Detective Markowitz adds. "How good is your memory? If we show you some books of mug shots, do you think you might be able to recognize him?"

The sound that comes out of my mouth is a kind of desperate wail, and it shocks me as much as it does everyone else in the room. "I can see it happening in my mind," I tell them. "It's almost like a movie, running over and over. He comes out of the back door and stands there, staring at me. And I know him. I know that I do. But I can't see his face!"

The detectives glance at each other quickly, then back at me. Johns rubs at an invisible spot on his chin. "Maybe it would help if you tried to describe exactly what you saw at the time," Markowitz says.

And Detective Johns adds, "Like what he was wearing. Jeans? A T-shirt? Maybe a white one?"

"Yes, jeans," I say quickly. "But not a T-shirt. It was kind of a plaid shirt—red, I think. Yes, red, but faded, and the sleeves were rolled up."

Markowitz is writing. "Very good. What else?"

"What else? Uh—he has a gun in his right hand." There's a long pause as I try hard to remember. "Help me!" I beg. "I have to know who he is. He killed my mother, and I hate him!"

Dr. Peterson gives me a quick look. I'm startled myself at the bitterness I can taste in my words.

"Take it easy, Stacy," Detective Johns drawls. "Just try to relax. We'll ask some questions, and see if you can come up with the answers."

He uses the telephone on the table next to my bed. The receiver almost disappears inside his hand. While he makes his call Markowitz asks me to go over the physical description I have given and try to add to it. He asks a lot of questions: Did I hear a shot? How close was I standing to the back door? Had I heard a car on the street before it all happened? And how old was the guy I saw?

"A few years older than I was," I tell him.

"Someone you knew at school?"

"No. Older. He goes—went—to high school."

"How old was he?"

I squeeze my eyes shut so tightly that they burn. "I should know!"

"He lives in your neighborhood? Your mother knew him, too?"

"Maybe. Oh, no. I don't think so. I don't know."

I try so hard, but I still can't see the murderer's face.

Finally Markowitz pauses. "I think that's it for now," he says.

"Wait. Let me ask you something," I say. "Why was this guy in our house? Why did he kill Mom?"

"It's listed as robbery," Markowitz answers. He looks at Dad, and Dad nods.

"He took my wife's wallet out of her handbag," Dad says. His voice rises as though he still couldn't believe what he's telling me. "And it was only ten or twelve dollars. She asked me that morning if I'd stop by the bank on the way home from work."

"Ten dollars? And he killed her?"

"One of the policemen who came after it had happened said he guessed the killer was someone looking for money to buy drugs, and he probably thought the house was empty. Maybe he panicked."

"Why did it have to be Mom?" I cry out. "Mom was gentle and loving and funny and kind. And she trusted everybody!"

Even when I was a very little girl, I wanted to be like Mom. But I wasn't like her at all. I'd get mad and shout and stamp, and Dad would march me off to my room to "think things over" and cool down. Thinking things over never seemed to help much.

Dad sighs. "Honey, we just don't know what was in the—murderer's mind. There's no way of knowing."

"We'll know when we arrest him!"

They look at me, and Markowitz says, "To make a solid case, the DA needs two kinds of evidence: an eyewitness to place someone at the scene of the crime and physical evidence that the person was there."

"I'm the eyewitness! I'm going to remember! I am! And you must have something from the house!" I think about some of the detective movies I've seen. "What about fingerprints? Could you look for fingerprints?"

Dad reaches down and takes my right hand. His forehead is wrinkled with worry. "Calm down, Stacy. Don't get overexcited." He looks at Dr. Peterson as though he were begging for help, but Dr. Peterson just gives a barely noticeable shake of his head.

"Granted, fingerprints can last for years," Markowitz tells me, "but chances are any fingerprints were cleaned up long ago."

I impatiently tug my hand away from Dad's. "But what about when the police investigated after Mom was murdered? Wouldn't they have taken fingerprints then?"

Markowitz nods. "We'll pull the file and see what they've got. There may be a chance they got some prints. Maybe even some clear ones. Obviously, if they had them, they didn't get a make on them; but maybe our boy's been in trouble since then, and we'll be able to match them. There may be some other physical evidence that may help. With luck they'll have the bullet that killed your mother. We won't know till we check it out."

"What good will the bullet do without the gun?"

"It might be worth something. It might not. It's our job to find out."

"Will you tell me? The minute you know?"

"These things take time," Johns says. He turns to Markowitz and mumbles, "Got a cigarette?"

The look Markowitz gives his partner is enough of an answer.

"Okay, okay, forget it," Johns says. He turns to me. "We'll try a computer search. May just luck out."

"Computer?"

Dr. Peterson smiles. "You've got a lot to catch up on, Stacy. Everyone does everything by computer now."

"What will happen to the murderer after you arrest him?"

"He'll go through all the legal processes," Johns says.

"Will he get the death penalty?"

Dad looks startled, but Johns takes the question as though he'd heard it over and over again. "Depends on the jury," he says. "In Texas the death penalty can be given if robbery, sexual assault, or kidnapping are associated with the murder. With this one we've got a robbery charge."

Markowitz tucks his notebook into his inside coat pocket. I get a glimpse of a gun in a shoulder holster. I remember another gun, and I shiver.

"I'm afraid we're tiring you," Markowitz says. As though they could read each other's mind, he and Detective Johns turn toward the door at the same time.

I climb out of my chair and walk a few steps with them. "I'm not tired. I won't get tired. I'll do anything I can to help you."

Markowitz hands me his card. "You can reach me through this number at any time. If you need us, don't hesitate to call." They stride from the room.

Dad follows them. So does Dr. Peterson. Because they've left the door open, I can hear the deep rumble of their voices, but only a word or two, so I stand just inside the door, where they can't see me.

"Well, yes, there is a possibility," Johns says. "But it's a slim one."

Dad is demanding. "But he could be a danger to Stacy."

There's a pause, and Markowitz answers, "Yes. It's a long shot, depending on where this guy is and whether he saw that newspaper article and how his mind works, but I suppose we could say there's a possibility that Stacy could be in danger."

"Then shouldn't we get protection for her?" Dad asks.

"If you don't mind, I'd like to butt in." Dr. Peterson

doesn't wait to find out if he can or can't and just goes on talking. "It's important that Stacy lead as normal a life as possible so that she can get all the pieces together."

"But I think—"

I don't hear the rest of what Dad says as they move farther away. I lean against the wall, waiting for Dad to come back to my room. I'm tired. I'm angry. And I'm scared because I don't know what will happen next. The guy without a face who murdered my mother. And Stacy McAdams. Who's going to find the other first?

Chapter Five

When Dad comes back to my room, he tries to hide his worries under a broad smile, but his eyes give him away. He hugs me again and mumbles against my hair, "Oh, Stacy, you can't know how wonderful it is having you back. You just can't know!"

It's warm inside Dad's hug. It's safe. "I don't want to stay in this clinic," I murmur. "I'm feeling all right now. Really. I want to go home with you."

He backs off and smiles at me. "Dr. Peterson says most likely you can come home the day after tomorrow. Only—"

When he doesn't finish his sentence, I ask, "Only what?"

For a moment he's silent. Then he says, "Only you'll be home alone, and I think someone should be with you."

I open my mouth to say, "But Mom will be there," and I have to remind myself that she won't. It's still so hard to believe. Dad is watching me, so I manage to stammer, "School. I have to go to school, Daddy."

Dad takes my hand and leads me to the bed, sitting beside me. "There are a lot of things to work out, Stacy.

And school is one of them. You were just finishing the seventh grade when all this happened to you. But your classmates are now in the eleventh grade. You aren't prepared for eleventh-grade courses, and naturally you won't want to go back to seventh grade. So maybe tutors? Home study? I don't know yet. It hadn't occurred to me to find out what to do."

"I don't want to go to school at home by myself."

Dad rubs a hand over his forehead and sighs. "No, no. Of course not. You'd be lonely."

"Maybe they'd let me take exams for the courses I was taking in seventh grade and make up eighth grade in summer school. That way I'd be in high school in the fall. I'll work real hard, Daddy, and not stay on the phone too long or watch too much television, and Mom will—"

The word enters us like an ache, and we just sit there, staring at each other.

"I—I'm sorry, Dad. I keep forgetting."

He puts an arm around me. "Honey, I still do. So many times I come home in the evening and for an instant actually expect Jeanne to call out to me."

"It hurts so much."

"Yes, it does."

"Will it ever stop hurting?"

"I don't know. We'll never stop remembering, but I don't know if the hurt will always be part of the remembering. I wish I could give you an answer that would help."

"If we had wishes, I'd wish none of this had happened. I'd wish we could go back. Have a second chance."

"Life doesn't give second chances, Stacy."

"Then I don't like life very much."

Dad's arm is strong, and he tightens his grip a little on my shoulder. "At some time or another everyone gets hit by problems that seem almost impossible to handle. You can give up without a fight, or you can climb over those problems and move on, because there are lots of good things ahead for you to discover."

"You make it sound too easy, Dad. Maybe you could do it, but I don't know yet if I can."

"You can." He makes a strange sound that startles me. I don't know if it's a laugh or a sob, so I twist to look at him. I can see the tautness of the muscles that are throbbing in his cheeks and chin. "Stacy, when Jeanne died, I wanted to run away, to hide, to do anything in order to escape all the pain."

"But you didn't."

"I did."

"I don't understand. You're here, Daddy."

"And I'll continue to be here with you, honey." I listen to footsteps pass my door and to someone laughing down the hallway. It seems a long time before Dad continues. "I drank a lot. Too much. It didn't help me escape anything. It just made it all worse. It was a stupid thing to do."

"Don't say you're stupid, Daddy! It wasn't your fault. It was the murderer's fault."

"You can't blame him for everything, Stacy. I'm certainly not going to blame him for something I chose to do."

"Well, I blame him. I hate him!"

"Hate isn't the answer. Think about your mother and what a forgiving person she was."

"I can't forgive him! I don't want to!"

He shakes his head sadly. I don't know why he can't understand how I feel.

"What we've been talking about is all part of growing up, of maturing," he says.

"Those are just words grown-ups like to use. Teachers say them. 'I expect you to be mature.' *Mature* doesn't mean anything."

"Yes, it does. It means a responsible way of looking at things, a more thoughtful way of making decisions."

"So if I grow up, then I'll automatically be mature."

"Stacy, I don't know how to explain it. It's something you'll feel inside. You'll find it out for yourself." He sighs. "Maybe your mother would have known how to explain these things to you."

I don't know what to say to him to make him feel better. I take his right hand and hold it tightly. "I love you, Daddy."

He gives his head a little shake, as though he were trying to toss away a lot of painful memories, and says, "I love you too."

The door slams open so suddenly that I gasp. Monty, the shaggy-haired orderly, bursts into the room, carrying my dinner tray. He must have startled Dad, too, because Dad jumps to his feet, standing between me and the orderly. "What are you doing?" Dad snaps.

"Well, hey, I got to deliver her dinner tray." Since Dad doesn't move, he says, "Here. You want it? You can give it to her. No problem."

Dad takes the tray, and as the orderly turns to

leave, Dad adds, "From now on, knock, and come in carefully."

"Hey, they know we're coming. We don't have to knock on doors around here."

Dad's voice is firm. "I said, from now on I want you to knock on this door before coming in. Understand?"

"Sure, sure," Monty says, and disappears.

Dad puts the tray on the bedside table. There's a deep pucker between his eyebrows, and he looks terribly tired. "I don't like that kid's attitude," he mutters.

"Daddy, he's okay. He's just always in a hurry. Maybe it's part of his job to get the trays around fast."

He looks at his watch. "I'd better grab a bite to eat pretty soon. It's almost time to get to the office."

"You have to go to your office? But it's so late."

"Uh, extra work," he says. The wrinkle between his eyebrows deepens as he looks at me. "Are you sure you'll be all right, Stacy?"

"Are you afraid something is going to happen to me?"

"No! Oh, no! I just meant, do you need anything? Can I do anything for you while I'm here?"

His glance slides away from mine. He's not telling me the truth.

"Better hurry, so you won't miss dinner," I answer. He holds me tightly in a big hug, then leaves, pausing at the door to give me one last, searching look and an attempt at a smile.

I'm staring at the dented metal top that covers the plate on my tray, wondering if I really want to take it off and find out what's under it, when a nurse with hair so red she looks like a lit candle pokes her head in the door. "Turn on Channel Two!" she says. "Quick!"

I move toward the television set that is mounted on the ceiling, but she bounces across the room and grabs a remote-control device that was lying behind a large box of tissues. She quickly presses buttons until she gets the right channel.

A man and a woman are tasting spaghetti and rolling their eyes with delight.

"It's going to be after this commercial," she tells me.

"What is?"

"You!"

I sit on the edge of the bed, wondering what she means. "There weren't any television reporters here."

"Oh, they were here. They just didn't get in to see you. The office put you under tight security."

"Security!"

"Oh, didn't they tell you that? There's a real cute off-duty policeman stationed in the hall to keep out the reporters and photographers. Norma's been walking by him so often she's wearing a path in the tiles."

"But what—"

She holds up a hand to hush me. "Listen. Here it is."

The newscaster is saying, "Stacy McAdams, Houston's sensational Sleeping Beauty, two days ago awakened from a four-year-long comatose state to announce that she is a potential eyewitness to a murder. However, she is just as inaccessible to reporters as the original Sleeping Beauty was to the rest of the world."

As he speaks the front door of the clinic is shown on

the screen. So that's where I am. It's a white one-story building that seems to ramble over a large area, and there are lots of pine trees shading it. There are people standing on the steps of the building and, on the grass, some of them carrying cameras. A policeman is facing them, his back to the closed doors.

On the screen appear the same two photographs that were in the newspaper.

"—called a model student by her teachers," the newscaster continues.

"Oh, no!" I groan. "That's not true. I wasn't a model student. I hated algebra. Anyhow, what he said makes me sound like a creep."

"You can't hear what he says if you don't keep quiet," the nurse answers, but a picture comes up of a group of protesters at the city hall, and the newscaster is off on another story.

The photographs of the two girls stay in my mind. Especially the one taken by the newspaper reporter. "Do I really look like that?" I whisper to myself.

The nurse hears me. "Sure you do! You're just as pretty as Sleeping Beauty was too! Remember the Walt Disney one, with her dark hair and big eyes?"

"That was Snow White."

She shrugs and laughs. "Doesn't matter. You're a really good-looking girl. You're going to have lots of dates and lots of fun."

She scurries out of the room. It's just as well, because I'm suddenly too surprised to talk to her. Dates? I don't know how to date. I don't even know what to say to a guy. Oh, sure, there were cute guys in my school, but Jan and I and my other friends didn't talk to them much, except when we worked up enough courage to say things like "You were real good in the game yesterday." And when they weren't around, we giggled a lot about them and talked about what we'd do if a guy wanted to kiss us. Suzie told us she'd been French-kissed, and she described what it was like and a lot more, but Jody kept yelling, "Yuck, yuck, yuck! That's gross!" so Suzie said we were babies and she wasn't going to tell us any more. We didn't care. We'd all read the same book Suzie had.

Jan and I asked our mothers when we could date, and they both said not until we were in high school. Jan and I made a real fuss about it. I guess now that was pretty silly, since none of the guys had asked us for dates.

Jan. Jan would know how to date, but I can't ask her what to do. She'd think I was really dumb. She's not the Jan I used to know, and I feel shy with her. Maybe I can ask Donna what to do.

I flop on the bed, nearly overturning my still-covered dinner tray.

From where I'm lying on the bed I can see the bottom edge of the door. It's open just a crack, just enough so that someone must be holding it open, just enough for someone to be watching me.

Quickly I scramble off the bed and manage to stammer, "Who—who's there?"

The door opens wide, and Monty blinks and grins. "Hey, it's just me."

"What do you want?"

"Your tray," he says. "I'm collecting them."

"You just brought it."

He shrugs. "Go ahead and finish," he says. He comes into the room, shoving the door so that it shuts behind him, and sprawls in the armchair. "Saw you on TV," he adds.

"You're not supposed to be in here."

"Gotta take a break once in a while. They really work us hard around here."

I grab the tray and shove it at him. "Here. Take it."

"You didn't eat anything. Aren't you hungry?"

"No."

He still doesn't move to take the tray. "You're a celebrity. You know that?"

"Go away."

Slowly Monty bends and curls as though it were taking a lot of effort to pull his body together and out of the chair. When he gets to his feet, he says, "You're not very friendly. I just thought it would be kind of interesting to ask you about what happened."

"I don't mean to be unfriendly. I just don't want to talk about it."

"You're scared. Right? But you don't have to be scared of me." He moves a step closer. "You can tell me. What did the guy look like? Do you know his name?"

I can't answer. I try to back up, but the bed is behind me. Only the tray is between us.

Monty's voice lowers. "It's sort of like a movie, you being the only one who can identify the guy who shot you and your mom. If it was a movie, you know the guy would come hunting for you, and it would probably be Jack Nicholson or somebody, and you'd try to hide out and—"

I drop the tray, and he hops backward, grabbing his left foot.

"Whadja do that for?"

"Get out of here!" I yell at him, and I jab at the call button.

A petite nurse with cropped black hair comes in as Monty is picking up the dishes and trying to wipe up the globs of food that decorate the floor.

"What's the matter?" she asks.

"She did it, not me!" Monty complains.

"I told him to get out! He kept trying to ask me questions!"

Monty stands, holding the messy tray. He grins at the nurse. "She's a celebrity. I just wanted to talk to her for a few minutes."

"Get back to your job," she says sternly. "You could get fired for deliberately annoying a patient."

She glares until he leaves the room. Then she smiles at me. "Don't mind Monty. He's not the brightest person around this hospital, but he's harmless."

"He wouldn't leave when I told him to. He frightened me. He asked too many questions."

"He was just curious," she answers. "Naturally the staff has been talking a lot about you, and he probably wanted to brag about getting some inside information. I'll tell the head nurse to chew him out, and he'll leave you alone. Want another dinner tray?"

"No, thanks. I'm not very hungry."

"Okay now?"

"I guess."

She leaves, and I sit on the edge of the bed, thinking about what happened. I guess I overreacted and got scared of Monty because I'm scared of so many things now. I don't want to be on television! I don't want a policeman guarding me in the hall! I don't want to be afraid anymore! I wish I were still thirteen!

I don't have time to think about Monty or policemen or anything else the next morning when the day snaps into place with doors banging open, blinds clattering up, breakfast, a shower, and Alice changing the dressing on my hip.

"Looks lovely," Alice says. "It's healing nicely. Dr. Peterson will be pleased."

"I'm pleased," I tell her.

Alice laughs. "That's taken for granted." She hands me a clean pair of jeans and a slightly faded T-shirt with a strange face on it. "This was my daughter's," Alice says. "I thought you'd like it."

"Is that your daughter's picture?"

Alice giggles. "No, honey. That's Glory Beans."

"Who's Glory Beans?"

"Why, she's—" Alice stops and stares at me with wide eyes. "Oh, my, I didn't think. You wouldn't know, would you? She's a very famous punk star. All the kids are crazy about her."

"Punk?"

"Whew!" Alice shakes her head. "I guess the best thing to do is bring you a four-year stack of newsmagazines, so you can catch up."

Mrs. Montez hops into the room as I pull the shirt over my head. "Fifteen minutes," she says. "I wrote your appointment on the schedule. Meet me in the physical therapy room on time!"

"Where is the—" But she's already galloping down the hall.

Alice gathers her tray of things and heads for the door. "Just turn left and go straight down to the main desk, then turn left again. It's at the far end of that wing. You can't miss it."

I go into the bathroom and brush my hair. It needs a trim. I could probably use a haircut, a new style. What are the new styles? Maybe there's a choice. Jan's hair looked good, not like that reporter's. I study my face. I'm getting a little more used to it now. It's not too bad. I wish my nose weren't so long and my eyes were bigger, but on the whole I kind of like this face. It's so much like the face I was used to seeing on Donna.

Quickly I get the lipstick from the drawer of my bedside table and run back to the bathroom with it. I smooth it on with my little finger. There. Maybe later I'll try some of the eye stuff. Not now. I remember Mrs. Montez's order to be on time.

As I enter the hallway I hear some voices to my right, down at what must be the nurses' station, but the hall to my left is empty. What happened to the policeman who was here? The hall is long, but at the end I can see a desk, or counter or something, and a lot of potted plants. That must be the main desk. Feeling like a six-year-old who's allowed to cross the street for the first time, I start down the hallway, following the directions Alice gave me.

Suddenly someone swoops up from behind me and grips my upper right arm. As I stiffen, digging in my heels and trying to pull away, a voice says, "What's with you? I'm just trying to help you escape the mob."

The voice belongs to Monty. He smiles at me, and I try not to stare at the wide gap between his front teeth.

I tug my arm out of his grasp. "What mob?"

"Down at the main desk."

As I take a skeptical look in that direction, he says, "Well, it's not exactly a mob, but a couple of reporters there are asking a lot of questions about you."

"I don't see anybody."

"They're by the main door. The cop is with them. If you go past them, they'll see you."

"I have to go by the main desk to get to the physical therapy room."

"Not if you use my shortcut. That's what I've been trying to tell you."

It makes sense. I don't want to have to talk to any reporters right now. So I shrug. Okay. Which way do we go?

He takes my arm again and pulls me down the hall to a swinging door, where he jerks me through. We're in a corridor that's narrower than the main hallway. I try to pull away. "You're hurting my arm. Don't squeeze it! And don't go so fast!"

"C'mon. You don't want to be late."

I nearly stumble, trying to keep up with him. The corridor turns, and I begin to realize that we're going in the wrong direction. We're heading toward what must be a back door to this building because in the upper half of the door is one of those crinkly-looking opaque glass windows, and I can see light shining through the window.

I grab his arm with my other hand, tugging and yelling, "Stop!"

When we're almost at the back door, he does stop, so suddenly it throws me off-balance. I bang into the wall, and the only reason I remain upright is that he's still hanging onto my arm. His eyes dart to each side as he nervously looks at the row of closed doors. "Don't make so much noise," he says.

"Let go of me!" I try to kick his leg, but he jumps aside.

His face is close to mine. I can smell the salty sweat on his forehead. "Hey, hold on. You'll get me in trouble if you don't shut up."

As I open my mouth wide to scream he claps a hand over it and in a low voice says, "Listen to me, will you? I'll get twenty bucks from one of the reporters if I bring you to the back door. The guy just wants to ask you a couple of questions and get a picture of you. That's all. You don't have to say much if you don't want. Okay? I mean I can really use the twenty bucks."

He takes his hand away from my mouth, and I spit and rub the back of my left hand over my lips, trying to wipe away the taste of his fingers.

"Well?" he asks.

"I don't think a reporter would do that."

"Look, who asks questions? Twenty bucks is twenty bucks." He smiles, as though he were trying to put me at ease; but his eyes narrow, and for an instant he looks away. I think he's lying.

Suddenly the knob of the back door rattles, and I look up to see a shadow through the glass. The door is locked, so the person on the other side gives up and presses against the glass, trying to see through it. The glass distorts his face into a monstrous blob with squashed nose and two dark spots for eyes. Can he see me? Those dark spots shift and seem to be staring in my direction. The doorknob rattles again.

Chapter Six

I yell at the top of my lungs, and now my kick connects with one of Monty's shins. He shouts an obscenity and grabs his leg. Two doors fly open, and people crowd into the corridor, squeezing behind and around each other, squishing Monty against the wall, where he squirms and struggles like a beetle on its back.

Maybe I don't make much sense, but I shout at everyone about what happened. The policeman arrives and dashes through the back door, but he comes back to say that whoever was at the door has got away. He grips the back of Monty's neck and marches him off.

Someone has an arm around my shoulders and is trying to calm me down. People are demanding, "What did she say? What happened?" But a loud, firm voice shatters the confusion.

"Now!" Mrs. Montez says, clapping her hands into the silence. "We are already well off schedule, and I will have no more of this silly chitchat in the corridor. We will all get back to work. Stacy, you come with me."

I follow her through a room that connects with one of the major hallways. Rubbing my arm where the orderly had held it, I ask, "If the man outside the door was a reporter, he would have stayed, wouldn't he? He wouldn't have run."

"Don't think about it," Mrs. Montez says without breaking her rapid pace. "That is the policeman's job. Your job is to pay close attention to what I will show and tell you."

We march into a room that is like a small health club with all sorts of exercise equipment, some of which I recognize, some of which I've never seen before.

"Did I use any of this?" I ask her.

"Of course," she answers. "How does your hip feel?"

"Alice says it looks good."

"I didn't ask how it looks to Alice. I asked how it feels to you."

"It's okay."

"Very good, Stacy. Then hop on the bicycle."

There is no question but that she should be obeyed. I can't imagine anyone ever questioning her authority. I begin to pedal, and she sets a timer. She acts like the queen of the world, but she's really not so bad. I can tell that she's made a shell to hide in so that people can't see that she really cares. But I look at the warmth in her eyes, and I know she does care. I pedal a little faster and glance at her and smile.

And I do pay close attention to what Mrs. Montez tells me. She's arranged for the loan of an exercise bicycle and insists that I also walk at least a mile or two a day. Believe me, I'm going to keep doing the exercises and stay in good shape because I've got a lot to do. First on my list: As soon as I can see the face of the guy with the gun and they catch him, I'm going to make sure he's convicted of murder.

The policeman comes by to report. Whoever was at the back door of the clinic was probably an inexperienced reporter who chickened out when the fuss began. Lots of apologies that I was upset, and please don't worry. No real problem, except for the orderly, who was in big trouble with the clinic manager.

I nod and make all the right answers, but something at the back of my mind keeps nagging uncomfortably that the orderly's answers were too easy. I don't believe it was a reporter. Why would a reporter use such sneaky tactics to meet me? But who else would it be?

Dad arrives to check me out soon after I get back to my room. Dr. Peterson joins us, and Alice comes in to help me pack. I am starting to get a little shaky, thinking about what it will be like to be back in our own house without Mom there too, when the phone rings. It's Detective Markowitz.

"They told me you were checking out. Will you be able to come downtown this morning to look through some mug shots?"

"Do you think that will help me remember?"

"It's worth a try."

"Then, I'll be there."

"Ask your father," he tells me, so I do.

Dad takes the receiver and talks to Markowitz. Then he turns to me. "Are you up to all this, Stacy? It's going to be an emotional strain."

I stand as tall as I can. "I can do it. I have to do it. I hate him."

"Hate isn't the answer, Stacy. It won't solve anything."

"It will send the murderer to prison. That's all I care about."

"There are other things to care about," Dad says, but then Norma and one of the other nurses crowd into the room to say good-bye and interrupt him. I hear Dad tell Markowitz he'll take me home first, then bring me to the downtown station. I gather up the rest of my things, wad them into a small suitcase Dad has brought, and say good-bye to the nurses and to Dr. Peterson.

"Take it easy, Stacy," Dr. Peterson says, and suddenly wraps me in an awkward hug.

I wish he hadn't. When he releases me, I stare at the floor and hope nobody notices my cheeks are hot. "He hugged me. Really!" I'll tell Jan, who thought he was gorgeous. But I suddenly remember that the Jan I want to tell doesn't exist anymore.

I just stumble close to Dad and hang onto his arm as Dr. Peterson smiles and says, "I'll see you in two weeks, Stacy. Just change the gauze pad on the incision each day, and call me if you have any problems."

We're met outside the front door of the clinic by a couple of reporters and cameramen. For a moment I can only stare at them.

"Not now," Dad says. He makes a shooing motion with the arm I'm not clinging to. "Stacy has nothing to say to you now."

We make a dash for the car.

Dad and I don't talk much on the way home. I can tell that he's trying hard to think of just the right things to say, and I am, too, so our wary words back off and circle each other. We make sense, but that's all you can say for our conversation.

I enter the front door of our house and walk past the living room back to the den. For a few moments I stand with one hand braced against the top of Dad's reclining chair. Everything looks the same. I wish it had changed. I wish someone had painted the walls blue, or bought a new chair, or put flowered pillows on the sofa —anything to make it different. It's just the way it was when Mom was here. Only Mom isn't here now, and she won't be back.

I glance around the room. "Where's Pansy?"

"Oh," Dad says, "I guess I forgot to tell you. Pansy just, well, disappeared last year. She was getting old. She—" He gulps, looking miserable, and quickly adds, "The Coopers have a cat that's going to have kittens soon. Maybe you'd like one of her kittens. We could ask. People usually want to get rid of—"

"Who are the Coopers?"

"They live next door, in the Hadleys' house. The Hadleys moved to Dallas a little over a year ago. You'll like the Coopers. They're a nice family. Three little girls."

I move to the window, studying the backyard, which is deep in the ragged color of spring. The grass needs mowing, and the althea bush is spewing limbs of lavender blossoms with abandon. The pink and white geraniums have overgrown their bed, and the confederate jasmine vine on the back fence waves loose tendrils in the breeze as though it were deranged.

In the large oak rests the funny little shack of boards, with its open door and oddly shaped windows, that Donna and I so carefully hammered together—with a little help from Dad. It had been my sanctuary, my quiet place, so many times in the past. I suddenly want to climb the oak and curl up in the tree house now. "It's been so long since I've been in the tree house," I murmur to myself.

But Dad is standing next to me and hears. "Don't climb up there, Stacy. It isn't safe now. One of the supporting limbs broke off in a storm, and the whole thing could come crashing down. I should have taken it apart long ago, but I just don't seem to have enough time."

I take his hand. "I'm sorry, Dad."

"It's not your fault, honey!" He suddenly brightens. "I've been talking to Donna and Dennis, and well, how would you like it if we set a date for all of us to drive down to Padre Island for a weekend? We know how much you always loved Padre Island. Remember? We used to go every year. I think it will be nice to have a family outing, don't you?"

The last thing I want to do is go to Padre Island. It holds too many memories, but Dad is looking so uncomfortable, so hopeful, that I smile and say, "Sure."

A worry wrinkle flickers on and off across his forehead as he asks me over and over again if I'm sure I'll be all right.

"I'm fine. Honest, I'm okay," I tell him. "Let's go see those mug books. The sooner the better."

It doesn't take long to get to Riesner Street, and on the way I gawk out the car window like a tourist. Downtown Houston is a collection of sharp-edged, shining new buildings which stretch high over their old, ornate brick neighbors like a collection of slender giants and chunky munchkins. Much of what I see is new to me, but the police station squats in a very old part of town and looks as though it had been there forever. Dad parks in the lot in front of the station. I climb from the car and stand there, staring at the building. All sorts of people are bustling in and out of the front doors.

"Would you rather go home?" Dad asks, and I realize that I'm visibly trembling.

I just shake my head and, clutching Dad's hand, blindly follow him into the building and across the lobby with its olive green asphalt-tile floors. There is a sudden crush of bodies as we enter the central room. Someone pushes against me. The shoulder of his plaid shirt is damp and sour with sweat as it rubs against my cheek. A woman who is bulging in her faded cotton dress follows the man, swinging sharp elbows and talking all the while in rapid Spanish. She treads on my toes.

"Ouch!" I mutter, and stare after her, but she's unaware of anything but her own problem. Beyond her two men are talking. A man in a business suit has his back to me, and a tall, light-haired guy, who is probably close to my age, faces me. For a second our eyes meet, but a fat character in khakis, puffing, muttering, and pushing between us, follows his protruding stomach through the crowd. An elderly woman and man come through one of the doors, clinging to each other, looking terrified. Are all these people here because they're in some kind of trouble?

"This way," Dad says. He leads me into the elevator and up to the second floor. Just down the hall is the homicide room and Detective Markowitz's office.

Markowitz tugs a handkerchief from his pocket and wipes the sweat from his face. "Air conditioner went out yesterday. Hot weather, even for Houston. Feels like midsummer already." He gives me one of those searching looks and asks, "Ready to get to work, Stacy?"

"I'm ready."

Markowitz seats me at a table at one side of the room and places five huge scrapbooks in front of me. Dad sits at the table next to me. "Take your time," Markowitz says. "Look at each face carefully. I'll be working here in the room most of the time. If you think you recognize the face in one of those photos, just call me."

"Okay," I tell him, and open the first scrapbook.

At first I'm hopeful, but by the time I've gone through the third book I'm discouraged. When I finish the fifth, I slam it shut with a groan.

Markowitz comes to the table. "No luck?"

"His picture's not in those books."

"Maybe it's there, but you can't remember him."

Dad stands up, the legs of his chair screeching against the floor. "I think this is enough for now. Stacy needs to get some rest."

"I'm not tired," I insist, but Markowitz looks at Dad and nods.

"She might need a little more time," he says. "Let's put it on the shelf for a few days."

"I'm going to remember," I tell them.

"I'm counting on it," Markowitz says. "But I'd like

to wait and have you remember the face naturally, instead of forcing your memory."

"How do you mean, *forcing* it?"

He looks at Dad again, then back at me. "Well, for one thing, I've given some thought to trying hypnosis."

"That's a great idea!" I grab Dad's arm. "Can you do it?"

"We've got some people in the department who are trained to hypnotize, and there are a number of M.D.s who can do it. But there's a big problem, and that is, it doesn't always hold up in court."

"But if I could remember—"

He shakes his head. "I'd like to catch this guy and see that he's put away so carefully there won't be any technicalities for a sharp lawyer to use like a key to get him out. Understand?"

I nod.

"So I'll get in touch with you next week," he says, and walks with us to the elevator.

We're in the same squeeze of bodies as we leave the building. I'm glad to get out of that place.

It's good to be home again. Dad was right. I am tired.

"Are you sure you don't mind staying alone?" Dad asks.

"Of course, I don't." I lie, so he leaves to go back to the bank where he works. The aching loneliness of the house soon creeps around me, clinging, crawling, trying to seep through my skin to the hollow inside of me. I push myself out of the deep armchair and hurry to the backyard.

As I walk to the center of our backyard I take a deep breath of the mingled sour-warm geraniums, honeyed jasmine, and spring-sharp air, remembering, remembering, and turn to face our house.

The screen door flies open, and someone races through. He pauses, stares at me—his pale eyes frightened and glittering—and raises the gun.

"No!" I shout, backing away in terror. He evaporates, and the memory turns as blank as unexposed film.

"I saw his eyes," I whisper, furious at myself for giving in to the fear that erased the face I was almost able to see.

I know I should walk that mile Mrs. Montez insisted on, but I'm reluctant to leave the house. Finally I find a book to read and settle back into the armchair, deliberately forcing myself to concentrate on the book. Slowly I manage to relax and curl into a cocoon of sound spun by the hum of the air conditioner.

The sudden jangle of the telephone smashes the silence of the late afternoon. I drop the book and jump from the chair, staring at the phone, wishing it would stop.

On the third ring I answer and sigh with relief and gratefully flop back into the chair as I hear Jan's voice. "Stacy! Your dad said you'd be home. I'm so glad!"

"I'm glad too," I answer, and wonder what to say next.

It doesn't matter because Jan says, "You're going to a party!" She doesn't give me time to answer but probably has guessed what my answer would have been because in one long breath she adds, "You've got to go, so don't say no. The party's being given in your honor.

Besides, it's important for you to meet some of the kids."

"Jan, I'm not ready to go to a party."

"You are too. You just don't know it."

"But everyone's different. I mean, they're like you. They've grown four years older, and—"

"Hey, Stacy, cut it out. We're friends. Remember? I wouldn't make you go to this party if I didn't think it was right for you, and it is. It's going to be Friday night at Tony's house. You know Tony. And he's got this great house that is super for parties, and everyone is going to be there. Not just the kids you remember. All sorts of people will be there. There always are at Tony's parties. I mean, most of them are really neat, but some—oh, well, I'll brief you on those, and they won't bother you anyway. All in all, it will be a great party."

"Jan, listen to me. I can't go. I haven't got anything to wear."

Jan sighs so elaborately I have to laugh. That dramatic sigh hasn't changed. "Everyone is wearing jeans. You have jeans. I know you have. You're going."

"I don't have a date."

"You don't need a date. It's not a date party. B.J. and I will pick you up at eight Friday night." She giggles. "That brings me to the best news of all."

"Jan, listen to me! That party's just the day after tomorrow. I'm not ready!"

"Hmmm," Jan murmurs. "That's partly true. I'm going to come over early and fix your makeup. We'll be there at seven, so don't argue anymore."

"You haven't given me much chance to argue."

"There. You see? It's all settled. And I've been talking long enough because you've got to come over to my house right away."

"Why?"

She giggles again. "Wait and see!"

"Jan?" But she's no longer on the phone.

The party's a dumb idea. I don't want to go. Who are these people now who used to be in the seventh grade with me? What are they like? Will they think I'm just a stupid kid?

I walk into the bathroom and study my face in the mirror. No, I'm not a stupid kid. "Who knows?" I say to the green-eyed girl who is staring back at me. "The party might be a lot of fun."

I grab my house keys and make sure the door is locked. It doesn't take long to walk to Jan's house, which is just a couple of blocks from ours; but the air is humid and sticky, and my shirt begins to cling to my back. My finger is still on the doorbell when the door flies open and Jan says, "Stacy, guess what?"

She takes a long look at me and rolls her eyes. "Thank goodness we have time!"

"Time for what?"

"You'll never believe this. No one will believe it. Jeff Clinton is coming over!" Jan grabs my arm and pulls me inside and down the hallway.

"Come on, Jan. Make sense," I manage to say. "Who's Jeff Clinton?"

"He's a guy at school," Jan says, "and we're talking real hunk. He comes to some of the parties, but he doesn't date. He told Bick once that there's a girlfriend in Michigan, where he came from, and they're sort of going steady, which makes this whole thing absolutely amazing. B.J. will die when she finds out!"

"Finds out what?"

Jan glides into the den with one of her elaborate sighs. "Pay attention, Stacy. I'm telling you. Jeff Clinton called me and said he'd be going to the party, and he'd like to meet you, and one thing led to another, and I said how about today, and he's coming over in a few minutes, so let's get some makeup on you."

"Jan! You fixed up a date for me?"

"It's not really a date. We'll just get acquainted and talk and drink some cola. And you and Jeff can get acquainted."

"Wait a minute!" I back away from her. "Why did he want to meet me?"

Jan's eyes open wider. "I don't know. Maybe he saw your picture in the paper and thought you were cute."

"That's not a good reason."

"Honestly, Stacy! That's as good a reason as any." She studies me, her head tilted to one side. "What's the matter? You look so—I don't know—suspicious. And that's silly. There will be lots of guys who will want to get to know you."

"But I want to know why."

Her mouth makes a large pink O. "I get it. It has to do with the guy you saw on your back porch, the one who—"

I interrupt. "Jan, I still can't see his face!"

"He wouldn't be Jeff. I told you, Jeff just moved here from Michigan last year. And anyway, you can't go around being suspicious of everybody."

I lean against the wall and sigh. "You're right. I guess I sound like some kind of nerd. It's just that—" Jan is looking at me with so much concern that I change the subject. "When he's here—Jeff, I mean—what am I supposed to do? I don't know what to say to him."

"Oh, you will." She tugs at my arm, dragging me into the bathroom. "Aren't you using the makeup kit I gave you?"

I shrug. "Sometimes."

"You're supposed to use it, Stacy! Look at you. Naked faces are not *in!*"

"In what?" I ask, trying to be funny, but Jan doesn't appreciate my humor. She's too busy doing things to my face.

The doorbell rings, and she hisses, "Here's the lipstick. Quick!"

"You answer the door," I tell her. "I'll put it on."

"Not much," she says as she runs from the room. "Just enough to count."

I stare at my reflection in the mirror, startled again by the girl who looks back. I like what Jan did. There's a kind of peach color over my eyelids, with a brown eyeliner. It makes my eyes look bigger. I fumble for the lipstick and put on just a little, following Jan's directions.

Taking a deep breath, I give one last glance at the mirror and head for the den, where I can hear Jan chattering.

As I enter the room a tall sandy-haired guy pulls himself up from Jan's father's reclining chair and faces me. His pale blue eyes crinkle at the edges as he smiles at me.

I can't help smiling back.

He's wearing snug jeans and sneakers without socks and a white T-shirt and a light kind of unbuttoned jacket with the sleeves pushed up to his elbows. It looks strange. It's probably another new style. He must work out a lot. I wonder if he's on the football team. His shoulders are broad, and even the jacket doesn't hide the muscles in his arms.

Jan introduces us and says, "Sit down, Stacy. I'll get something for us to drink."

Suddenly I'm shy. I clasp my hands together and stare at them, wishing I knew what to talk about to a guy.

"Have you thought yet about going back to school?" Jeff asks. "Will they let you make up some of the classes in summer school?"

I'm so thankful that he didn't ask me about Mom or the murderer that I stumble all over myself answering his question. "Dad and I were talking about that. I don't know what they'll want me to do. I do know one thing. I can't go back to junior high school. I'd be so much older than everyone else." I stop for breath. "What I'd like to do is study the things I've missed. I could study hard and make up some of the work. If they'll just let me."

Jeff smiles. "It's hard to study alone. Maybe some of the kids could help tutor you and get you ready for exams. If you could pass exams, they might give you credit for the courses."

"That's a great idea."

"I'll volunteer to be a tutor. I'm pretty good in math."

"Really? You'll help me learn the math I've

missed?" Maybe it's excitement. Maybe it's the way he's leaning forward just a bit, looking at me as though I were the most interesting person he's ever seen. I feel myself blushing.

Jan comes into the room, balancing a tray with three glasses of cola and a plate of chocolate marshmallow cookies. She remembered. They're my favorite.

Jan looks at my red face, and one eyebrow rises and falls.

But Jeff starts talking about how much he likes math and how he once tried building a computer, and it gives me a chance to calm down. Afternoon sunlight tilts through the window next to him, highlighting his face. I study it, liking it. For some reason Jeff seems much older to me. I can't explain it. Maybe it's something I see in his eyes. He seems more knowledgeable, more aware than kids his age should be. Strangely I have the feeling that I've seen him before. It can't be, but there's something familiar, something I should remember. I don't know what it could be.

The conversation has shifted to the party. I don't know most of the people Jan is rattling on about, and Jeff begins to look kind of bored.

He stands up and smiles at me. "I'd better go, Stacy. If you'll check into the books you'll need for algebra and geometry and get an okay from one of the counselors, we'll start on the tutoring anytime you say. I can come over to your house every afternoon and work with you."

Both of Jan's eyebrows go up this time, but I don't think Jeff notices. He's looking at me. Jan dashes into the kitchen, so I walk to the front door with Jeff. "I appreciate it, Jeff. I really do."

He smiles again. "See you at the party," he says, and walks to his car. It's a plain vanilla gray sedan and looks like the cars I remember, so it's probably four or five years old.

"Stacy!" Jan hisses, and I realize I'm still standing in the open doorway, watching Jeff, so I close the door and hurry back to the den.

"He likes you!" Jan shouts. "It's obvious instant infatuation! B.J. will go out of her mind!"

"He just offered to tutor me in math," I tell her.

"Math is as good an excuse for seeing somebody as any other excuse," Jan says. She's so pleased with herself that she practically purrs.

The clock in her den chimes five times. I automatically count along with it. "I'd better go home," I tell her. "Say hi to your parents for me."

"Mom will be disappointed that she missed you. She didn't know you'd be here. She keeps asking me how soon you'll be able to come over for dinner."

"As soon as possible. Your mom is a great cook."

Jan opens the front door and calls to me when I reach the sidewalk, "I'll see you tomorrow! This is going to be some party!"

When I get home, I poke through the refrigerator. I never really learned to cook. Oh, well, I can make grilled cheese sandwiches for dinner.

Donna and Dennis come over, and Donna says next time I have to go back to the police station she'll go with me since Dad doesn't think he can take any more time off his daytime job, and Donna has only one class and can skip it.

That's when I find out that Dad has been holding down two jobs, so he can pay all my medical bills. I hate the guy who murdered Mom even more.

I wish so hard I could see his face. How do I explain to Dad or to Detective Markowitz about my weird feeling that if I don't discover the identity of the murderer pretty soon, I may run out of time?

Chapter Seven

Early-morning mists from the Gulf slither inland, mingling with the pollution from the northeast factories and refineries, giving us a day that's gray and grimy with smog.

Donna arrives, waddling smugly. She puts a covered bowl into the refrigerator. "The baby kicked all night," she complains, but she looks delighted. She studies the green cotton shirt and jeans I'm wearing. "We're going to Foley's this morning. You have to get some clothes that fit you, Stacy."

"When do you want to go?"

"As soon as the store opens."

Later, all the way to Foley's Memorial store, she chats about the kinds of clothes I'll need: jeans and shirts. I feel comfortable with those. But she gets me a couple of dresses, and they're weird.

"I wouldn't buy you a 'weird' dress." Donna is firm. "You just don't know anything about the styles for your age yet. Trust me."

"You're being bossy," I tell her as she pulls out Dad's charge card. "You're trying to act like Mom, but Mom wasn't bossy."

"I'm trying to help you." Donna looks at me the way she used to when I'd yell at her that it wasn't fair she always beat me at Monopoly.

I take a deep breath. "I'm sorry. I didn't mean it." I really don't care about the dresses. What to wear is just one more stupid thing to have to get used to, and right now it seems unimportant.

Donna buys some bras, panties, and a slip. She decides that I've got everything I'll need for a while, so she drives me home.

I dump my packages on the sofa in the living room.

"I'll hang them up for you," she says.

"I can do that myself."

"Better do it now, so the dresses won't get wrinkled. I promised Dennis I'd call him before I started home."

As she heads toward the kitchen phone I scoop up my packages, take them to my room, and drop them on the bed.

A persistent pat-pat on the window greets me. It's a loose branch of a scraggly, climbing Queen Elizabeth rose. I open the window, soaking in the pungent-sweet smells of the garden, the sounds of a dog barking down the street, and the laughter of the children in the yard next door. The Cooper children. They don't see me, so I watch them play.

The two younger girls are playing tag. The older girl—Donna said she was twelve—leans against the solid trunk of their old elm tree, laughing at her sisters, yelling encouragement to the little one, who's trying so hard to catch her sister. They're look-alikes, with round freckled faces and light brown hair.

For an instant I ache to join them. The twelve-year-old—she looks almost thirteen—would be close to my age. She might like to be friends and—

But I'm no longer thirteen. I turn and see myself in the full-length mirror that hangs on the door. I'm seventeen, in a world I don't want, that I'm not ready for. I bang my fists against the wall. *You, with the gun—whoever you are, I hate you. I hate you!*

"Stacy."

I hurry back to the front hallway to join Donna, who's fishing in her handbag for her car keys. She has to go, and I have to let her. I fight the fear I know will come with the lonely house.

"Are you sure you'll be all right by yourself?" she asks as she studies my face.

I take her by the shoulders and laugh, trying to sound braver than I feel. "I'm a big girl now. Remember?"

She smiles and hugs me. As she presses against me the baby moves, so I feel it too. I want to keep holding her, so that I can feel the baby again, sharing it with her. But Donna steps back and says, "If you need me, just call. Oh—there's a chicken pasta salad in the refrigerator."

"Thanks for everything, Donna. Thanks for shopping for me."

"If you decide you really don't like the dresses—"

"They're great," I say. "Go on. You've got things to do." The longer she stays, the harder it will be to let her leave.

"The blue one is especially—"

"I love it! Get going!"

I throw open the front door and shriek at the face that's staring bug-eyed into mine.

"Oh, dear!" the woman on our front porch says. She brushes back the brown bangs that hang over her eyes and pushes her oversize glasses up on her nose. "I didn't mean to startle you! I saw you come home a few minutes ago, and I was just going to ring the bell."

Donna steps up beside me and holds out a hand. "Mrs. Cooper, you must come in and meet Stacy." She turns to me. "Remember, Stacy? I told you that Mrs. Cooper and her family live next door."

We say all the right things to each other as Donna moves us into the living room.

"I can't stay," Mrs. Cooper says. "I just wanted to greet Stacy and tell her the entire neighborhood is glad she's back and feeling good again."

"Thank you," I say.

"Oh, I know we weren't here before; but we're so fond of your family, and that includes you too."

"Thanks."

"And I am planning to send over a casserole or something. It's just that I've been so busy with the little girls, and you do understand, I know. It's just PTA and the church society and dental appointments and one blessed thing after another. You certainly are a pretty girl."

"Thank you."

"So much like Donna."

"Yes. Thanks."

She hardly pauses for breath. "I was wondering if you'd baby-sit my girls this evening. One of my husband's clients invited us out to dinner—at the last minute, wouldn't you know?—and we'd need you for just a short time. Could you make it seven o'clock? We promise to be home by ten, so you won't get too tired."

Donna holds up a hand. "But Stacy is—"

I interrupt her. I don't want to tell Donna that I'm still feeling jittery about being alone in the house. I'd just as soon Donna didn't know. "I'll be glad to baby-sit," I tell Mrs. Cooper. "I don't have anything I have to do tonight. Sure. I'll be there."

"Maybe we should ask Dad," Donna says.

Mrs. Cooper manages to look both puzzled and horribly disappointed at the same time. "But it's just right next door," she says. "And the girls are all well behaved."

"Dad will be at work anyway," I tell Donna, and I smile reassuringly at Mrs. Cooper. "See you at seven."

Mission accomplished, she's off and away, and Donna leaves after one more reassuring hug.

I start puttering around in the kitchen, reading cookbooks as though they were messages from a secret power and I were a decoder with the CIA. Why didn't I ever learn to cook anything besides fudge? I peek inside the bowl of chicken pasta salad that Donna made. What's a pasta salad? It sounds terrible.

To my surprise I find a recipe for a casserole that seems to match up with the carrots and onions and ground beef I pull out of the refrigerator. That's such a good start I tackle the putting-together part with real enthusiasm. After it's been in the oven awhile, it starts to bubble and actually smells good. I'm really proud of myself.

I carry the little TV set to the kitchen and listen

while I'm setting the table. It's the local news, and the newscasters talk about a rapid transit system and things I don't know anything about. Then I hear my name and look up to see that scene outside the clinic. Did I really feel as scared as I look? Yes. I guess so. But they're off now on a story about a convenience store shooting. A couple of times I glance at the telephone. I wish it would ring. I wish it would be Jeff. But the telephone is silent.

Dad comes home, kisses me, and says, "I think I'll just settle down with the newspaper for a few minutes before dinner's ready."

I make a lettuce salad, but according to the timer, we have fifteen minutes to wait for the casserole. So I join Dad in the den. He's asleep in his chair, the newspaper spilling from his lap. Carefully I pick up the classified section. It gives me an idea.

As I turn the pages they rustle. Dad's eyelids flicker, then open. He smiles at me. "Guess I had a little nap." He sits up, stretches, then notices what I've been reading. Before he can say a word, I speak up.

"I want to get a job."

"Stacy, we talked about your catching up on your schoolwork."

"I can do both. I'll study hard, Dad. I know how much work I've got to make up. But there's no reason I can't get a job too. I want to help."

"It will be too much for you. We won't discuss it."

"We have to discuss it!"

He sighs. "Stacy, I'm afraid you got your stubbornness from my side of the family, but maybe that's good because I can be as stubborn as you can." Dad smiles, and I know he's trying to ease things between us as he says, "I remember once when we met head-on about whether or not you were old enough at twelve to go on a date, and your mother said the two of us were like that pair of rams in the Disney movie, banging their heads to the tune of the 'Anvil Chorus.'"

"You won that argument," I say.

"I'm going to win this one too."

"I just want to help. You work at the bank in the daytime and do bookkeeping at night, and it's too much."

"We won't discuss it."

"You already said that. You make me so mad, Daddy! All I want to do is talk to you!"

He sits up and leans toward me. The lamplight in the room casts shadows that deepen the hollows under his eyes. "Honey, I want to talk to you too," he says. "I want to talk to you about your mother."

My shoulders are stiff, and there's a tight place at the back of my neck that begins to throb. "There's nothing to talk about."

"Yes, there is. I'm worried about you because you haven't mourned her."

"Yes, I have."

"I think you're holding your feelings in, afraid to let go and face what happened. That's not good, Stacy."

I can't tell him about my feelings. How can I explain about the burning fingers of hatred that claw at my mind?

The oven timer buzzes, so I scramble to my feet. "Dinner's ready!"

He studies me for a moment, then says, "Okay,

Stacy. Just remember, when you're ready to talk, I'm ready to listen."

There isn't anything I want to say now. There's too much to think about to wonder about my feelings. That will come later.

Dad praises me over and over for the wonderful casserole. I think it tastes a little flat, but he has second helpings, so I suppose he really likes it. I tell him I'm going to baby-sit the Cooper kids. He starts to frown but changes it to a smile and says it's all right. Maybe he's got a limit of one argument going at a time. Maybe he thinks he'll have his say about the big things and let the little things go by. Who knows what parents think?

After the dishes are finished and Dad has left, I make sure I've got Detective Markowitz's card in my pocket. I leave the lights on in the den, lock the house carefully, and cross the lawn to the Cooper house.

Mrs. Cooper opens the door. She reminds me of one of those dust devils that whirl across the open lands in Texas as she darts and swoops into the den, introducing me to Keri, Meri, Teri, and Mr. Cooper. She points out the emergency numbers in the kitchen and the phone number where they can be reached. Then she disappears for a moment into a closet, emerges with a handbag, bobs over her daughters with a good night kiss, and is out the door, carrying her balding and bemused husband with her.

The girls stare at me.

"Help me get your names straight," I tell them, knowing that it had to be their mother who had named them.

"Think of it as alphabetical," the oldest one says. "K before M and M before T. I'm Keri. I'm twelve."

Teri, who looks as though she were about six, pipes up. "Mom said you're the Sleeping Beauty. Are you the real Sleeping Beauty?"

"No," I say. "That's just a make-believe story." I glance around the room. It doesn't look a thing like it did when the Hadleys lived here. Everything is flowered chintz with red poppies and ruffles. A big bouquet of matching artificial flowers is on an end table, and dozens of photographs of the girls are on the wall over the sofa. The wall has been paneled in a light birch wood. How can this house look so different when our house looks so much the same?

On the floor, nearly covering a round scatter rug, are Barbie dolls, dresses, houses, cars—the whole works. I wonder where Daddy put my Barbie dolls. Maybe they're packed away.

"You've got a lot of clothes for your dolls," I tell the girls. "Do you care if I look at them?"

"Wanna play?" Meri asks.

I shrug. "Why not?"

We sit near the edges of the rug, and in a few minutes I'm putting a red net ball gown on one of the dolls, and Keri's doll is driving over to visit mine.

"Three movie stars are going to be at the dance," Keri's doll says.

"Who cares about movie stars?" my doll says. "Have you heard? The duke of York is going to be here."

"And I'm going to sing with the band," Meri's doll says. "I'm a famous singer."

"You sing like a frog," Keri says, and we all giggle.

The game goes on until Teri steps in the middle of the rug and stamps her foot. "Nobody listens to me! I tried to tell you what I saw upstairs!"

"You were upstairs?" I'm startled and worried, because I didn't realize she had left the game.

"I told you I was going to the bathroom!"

"I'm sorry, Teri. Sit down. Our dolls are going to the beach. Do you want the purple bathing suit for your doll?"

"No! If you're not going to listen to me, then I won't tell you."

I put out my arms to her and pull her down on my lap. "Hey, I'm sorry. I'll listen. What do you want to tell us?"

"About somebody who's in your yard. I looked out the window upstairs, and I saw somebody trying to look in your windows."

We all jump up. Meri screeches, and I shush her. "We don't want him to hear us. We'll have to be quiet."

But we race upstairs, ahead of Teri, who's now filled with her own importance. She joins us in the dark room and leads the way to the wide bedroom window that overlooks our house and yard.

"Look," she whispers.

I lean over the heads of the three girls, straining to differentiate between the shapes and shadows. One shape moves, and I see it step back from the side of our house, where it has apparently been trying to see into my bedroom window. In an instant it has slid through the darkness and disappeared around the back of the house.

Keri clutches my arm, and I feel her tremble as she whispers, "He's in your backyard! Stacy, what if he gets inside your house?"

Chapter Eight

I step back from the window, pulling the children with me, and try to sound calm. "We'll call the police. They'll take care of it."

"I want my daddy!" Meri is so terrified that Teri puckers up and begins to wail. That sets Meri off, and it takes me a few minutes to quiet them down, so that I can make the telephone call to Detective Markowitz.

The woman who answers my call tells me that Detective Markowitz is not there, but she'll get in touch with him, so I explain why I'm calling. She says that she'll send a squad car out to investigate, then try to reach Markowitz.

The Cooper children and I huddle together in the living room, where we can press our noses against the picture window and watch for the police car to arrive. Maybe one of us should stay at the upstairs window and watch for the shadow to appear again, but we're all too frightened. We want to stick together.

"Let's call Mama," Teri says. Her lower lip wobbles, and I hug her tightly.

"In a few minutes," I tell her. "It will be safer if the

police check things out before your mother and daddy get home."

"They said they'd be home by ten," Keri answers, "and it's almost ten."

"You were supposed to put us to bed at our bedtime," Meri accuses. "Mama's going to be mad at you."

"So you want to go to bed right now?" I ask her. She shakes her head vigorously.

"I want Mama," Teri whimpers.

Maybe I expected sirens and screeching tires, something like what I've seen in police movies. But a police car comes quietly down the street and parks in front of the Cooper house. Two policemen climb out. One stays in the yard, studying our house next door, and one comes to the Cooper front door.

I nearly trip over Teri, who dashes under my feet as I run to open the door, but I manage to hang on to her and tell the officer what happened.

Teri keeps interrupting, shouting, "I saw him first!"

"Just stay put and keep the door locked," the officer says. "We'll look around."

He shuts the door firmly. We rush to the large window again and see him and his partner walk toward our house, flashlights sweeping a crisscross pattern of light ahead of them. In a few seconds they are out of sight.

"Let's go upstairs and watch out the bedroom window," Keri says.

She tries to squeeze past me, but I grab her arm. "No! We're safer here. The policeman told us just to stay put. Remember?"

There's a little brass clock on the mantel, and it chimes ten times. It's not just the Coopers who are due home at ten. Dad told me that he usually gets home a little after ten o'clock too. I don't want them to come now. Not with whoever it was prowling around our house! What if someone gets hurt?

The telephone's ring is so shrill that we all jump, and Meri screams.

"It's just the phone," I say, but they cling to me and shove against me as I hurry to answer it. We're like a pack of puppies, bumping and pushing against each other.

Just after the third ring I manage to grab the receiver before Keri can snatch it.

"What's up?" Markowitz asks me. "Where are you?"

I fill him in, and he says he'll be right over. "Tell the officers to stay until I get there," he adds.

The sound of his voice is like a pat on the back, an arm around my shoulders. "Everything's going to be all right," I tell the girls. "Let's go back to the window."

As we reach the front window and settle against the glass, one of the officers appears, cutting across the lawn. He comes to the front porch and rings the bell just as the Coopers' car pulls into the driveway.

"Oh-oh," Keri says.

Oh-oh is right. As I open the door Mrs. Cooper flies across the lawn, screeching, "What happened to my children?"

"It's all right, ma'am," the officer says, and at the same time Teri shouts her story at the top of her lungs. Meri rushes into her mother's arms, crying loudly, and Keri yells that there's a prowler outside and everybody should get in the house and lock the door.

The perpetually puzzled Mr. Cooper appears, and Dad, who has also just come home, and the other officer join the scene.

"Let's all be quiet," Dad says in a loud, firm voice as he checks out everyone in the group, "so we can find out what's going on."

Apparently Mrs. Cooper has been counting noses, too, and is satisfied with the tally, so she's ready to listen. Miraculously she is able to quiet her children by firmly saying "Hush." I wonder if there's an unspoken "or else" behind it.

One of the officers explains about my call. "But we couldn't find anyone in your yard," he adds to my father. "The windows all seemed to be locked, and both the front and back doors were secured."

The other officer speaks up. "Could be your daughter is a little nervous. Can't blame her. And people sometimes think they see things in the dark, things that aren't really there. You know, shadows and tree branches moving in the wind, stuff like that."

"But we all saw him," Keri says.

"I saw him first," Teri shouts.

"It was a 'him'?" Mrs. Cooper asks Teri. "A boy? A man?"

Teri thinks for a moment. "Maybe it was a monster."

There's a pause, during which the adults all look at each other. Then the first police officer says, "There's no one there now," in the tone of voice that implies he doubts there ever was. He turns to Mrs. Cooper. "We checked your yard out, too, ma'am, just to be sure."

"Thank you," she says, takes a deep breath, and

immediately begins to order her children inside, ask i
they've brushed their teeth, why they aren't in thei
pajamas, and have they completely forgotten the rul
about picking up their toys before they go to bed?

I just quietly shut the door and leave with Dad and
the policemen. Mrs. Cooper didn't remember to pay
me, but it doesn't matter. I wasn't a very good baby
sitter, and I'm not going to baby-sit again—not until th
murderer is found and he's in prison. I don't know wha
happened tonight, if anything, but if I'm in any danger
I don't want to involve anyone else.

Markowitz arrives and talks to the policemen.
They leave, and he checks out the yard himself with
high-powered flashlight. He bends and stoops and ex
amines the ground under each of the windows as Da
and I follow along behind him. "If we'd had some rair
we might have been able to get a footprint," Markowit
finally says, snapping off his light and tucking one end o
it into the pocket of his jacket. He thinks for a momen
then looks carefully at me.

"Stacy, I think it was a false alarm."

"We saw someone."

"Male or female?"

"I don't know. I couldn't tell."

"Why?"

"It was too dark. It was just a shadow."

He shakes his head and says, "That's what I mear
It is dark tonight, too dark to know what you saw. I'r
inclined to think it was too much imagination."

Dad puts an arm around my shoulders and lets ou
a sigh. "I thought so, but I'm glad to hear you say i
Would you like a cup of coffee, Mr. Markowitz?"

"No, thanks," Markowitz says. "This was a long day. I'm beat." He walks with us to the front door. "Want me to check inside?"

"Do you think you should?" Dad asks.

"Nope. Your house was locked up tight. We would have found signs of forced entry if anyone had tried to get inside." Markowitz smiles at me. "Take care, Stacy. I'll be in touch with you soon."

Dad seems satisfied, and so does Markowitz, but I'm not. "What if—" I begin, then don't know how to say what I'm thinking without getting Dad all upset.

But Markowitz knows, and he answers. "Nothing's going to happen to you, Stacy. We'll watch out for you. You're our star witness."

Is that all he cares about? That I might be able to testify against whoever killed my mother? Maybe that's all that would matter to me, too, if my job were trying to catch criminals. He's smiling, but I don't trust his smile because I don't believe everything is as simple as he makes it out to be. I know that I saw someone prowling around our house tonight, and nothing Markowitz or the other officers have said is going to make me change my mind.

I don't sleep well. In spite of the air conditioning, the air is sticky and clammy, and the sheets are a tangle around my legs. I doze and wake, alert to every little pop and creak of the house. Somewhere nearby the sharp trill of a mockingbird shatters the dark, and my eyes fly open. What is it? What?

Every time I close my eyes I see the screen door open, the hand raise the gun, the face—I can't see the face! I know I'm trying too hard, but I've got to be able to see it.

At breakfast the next morning I tell Dad I'm going to make an appointment to talk to the counselor at Glen Creek High School, and I tell him about the party tonight.

Dad looks uncomfortable. "When Donna was your age, your mother took care of those things," he says. "I can't remember all the questions I'm supposed to ask." He thinks for a moment, then brightens. "Who will you be going to the party with?"

"Jan and B.J."

"I know Jan, but who's this guy B.J.?"

"Dad, B.J. is a girl. You met her—a long time ago. And it's not the kind of party where you have to come with a date."

"Will this party be supervised?"

"I don't know."

"Well, do you know where it will be?"

"Tony Maconda's house."

"Do you know him?"

"Sure. I've known him since kindergarten. His family used to live just a couple of blocks from us, and then his father got to be vice-president or something in the oil company he worked for, and they moved to one of those big houses near the bayou."

There's something else I should remember about Tony, something nagging my mind, but for now I can't think of it. I do remember that he got caught shoplifting once, and there was one day when he bragged he had marijuana in his locker, only that time he didn't get caught. I used to think Tony was a creep. But then, I thought Bick was, too, and Jan says he's wonderful. People change a lot in four years.

I tell Dad, "Tony's short and plump and—" I lean back in my chair. "Oh, Dad, I don't know what he looks like now!"

"Okay, Stacy. I know who you mean. I've met Tony's parents. They seem like reasonable people."

He stares at the table, and I know he's trying to think up the other questions he's supposed to ask, but I'm tired of this. I hadn't wanted to go to the party, but now it's become a challenge. There's no reason why Dad shouldn't let me go with Jan.

"At seventeen I should be old enough to make up my own mind about going to a party!"

"It's just that you're not quite used to the world as it is now," he says. "There's a problem with drugs and—"

"Daddy!" I interrupt. "Kids were taking drugs when I was thirteen! And you don't have to worry about me. I'm not dumb enough to take drugs."

He reaches across the table and takes my hands. "Stacy, I wasn't intimating that you'd take drugs. I was —oh, honey, I want to protect you, and I don't know how to do it."

I squeeze his fingers and smile at him. "Daddy, you're doing a good job of protecting me. Just don't overdo it. I've got to be allowed to grow up."

He nods and tries to smile back. "Well, you'll be with Jan. She's a good girl. And I know where you'll be. What time are you leaving for the party?"

"Jan's going to be here at seven to help me get ready."

He looks puzzled. "Do you need something special to wear?"

"No, Dad. It's informal. I'll wear my jeans. Jan's going to help me with my makeup."

"I feel so lost," he says. "I wish your mother were here."

I fight back the hot pressure behind my eyes, answering, "I wish she were here too," and adding quickly, "but you're doing a great job, Dad. And Jan will be glad to see you."

He carries his coffee cup and empty cereal bowl to the sink. "Not tonight, I'm afraid. I almost forgot to tell you. I'll get a hamburger for dinner because we've got to go over some reports that came in from one of the branches. It's going to mean that I'll be there later than usual, maybe until eleven or even midnight."

"I may get home before you do," I tell him.

He bends down to kiss my forehead. "Have a good time at the party, Stacy."

"Thanks," I answer, wishing I didn't have to go.

In the afternoon a delivery truck comes with an exercise bicycle.

The moment the deliveryman leaves the telephone rings. "Is everything all right, Stacy?" It's Mrs. Cooper's voice.

"Yes. Everything's fine."

"Well, you know how it is in a neighborhood—everyone checking on everyone else, and I saw a delivery truck, so I thought—" She interrupts herself to tell me about some friends who had a delivery truck parked in their driveway, and none of their neighbors thought a thing about it, except it really wasn't a delivery truck, and most of their furniture was stolen.

"This one was a real delivery truck, and it brought my exercise bicycle," I tell her.

"I guess I'm just being too careful," she says. "But one thing and another, like that excitement last night and that same car that seems to be cruising this street, although my husband says I'm just looking for trouble, and—"

"What car?" I have to interrupt.

"I don't know," she says. "Just a car. Next time I see it I'm going to write down the license number."

"How often have you seen the car?"

"Oh, three or four times."

"What kind of car is it?"

"Goodness, I have no idea."

"What color is it?"

"Plain. You know."

"Brown? Blue?"

"Yes. Something like that. Nothing special."

There's no point in asking her any more questions. Besides, the car she saw is probably no more a threat than the delivery truck that brought my bicycle.

"One more thing." Mrs. Cooper continues by telling me she's sorry she forgot to tell me about the girls' bedtime, and she's sorry we all got so excited. She forgot to tell me that Teri has an overactive imagination, and she apologizes for forgetting to pay me for babysitting. If I come over tonight or tomorrow, she'll have the money for me. By the time we end our conversation I feel like gasping for breath.

I climb on the bicycle and follow all of Mrs.

Montez's instructions, working up a real sweat. Next
comes a steamy, hot shower. I feel good, really good.

As I turn off the shower I hear the telephone ringing. Wrapping the towel around myself, I run to answer
it. How long has it been ringing? Whoever is calling
must know that I'm home. Maybe it's Donna or Dad.

"Hi," I gasp into the receiver.

A whispering voice hisses, "What do you remember, Stacy?"

"Who are you?" The whisper is weird, but I'm too
shocked to be frightened.

"It's been a long time," the voice says. "Why don't
you just forget? It would be safer for you to forget."

I hear my own voice as though I'd stepped outside
my body and were looking and listening to someone
else. I expect to be afraid, but I'm not. It's as though I
were made of glass, with a red, churning anger bub-
bling up inside me. Words drop like chunks of molten
glass as I ask, "Are you the one who killed my mother?"

The whisperer doesn't answer for a while, so I ask
again, "Are you?"

The voice over the telephone is softer now. "I
heard that you don't remember my face."

"But I will," I say.

"Then I'll have to do something about it."

"Not if I find you first."

There's a pause, then a chuckle. It sounds almost as
though he were talking to himself. This guy is weird. I
can't make out the first few words, but I hear him say
". . . have a friend."

I interrupt. "What are you talking about? What
friend?"

"You haven't got a chance, Stacy," he whispers.

There's a click as the line goes dead. Slowly I put down the receiver. I didn't know that hate could be this strong. He has torn up my life. He's destroyed four years that belonged to me. And most horrible of all, he's taken my mother away from us. I shiver as I realize I actually hate him enough to kill him.

Chapter Nine

The late-afternoon sun is rapidly being swallowed b
dusky shadows, so I hurry through the room, fumblin
with trembling fingers, turning on a couple of lamp
The light helps. And the movement brings everythin
back to normal. I think about the person who made tha
telephone call. Why did he laugh and talk to himself
He might have been high on something, some weir
character who was playing games. Our telephone num
ber's in the phone book, easy for anyone to find, an
there are a lot of crazy people who might think a ca
like that was funny. No. I'm sure he wasn't the mu
derer. The murderer wouldn't call me. Of course, h
wouldn't.

The doorbell rings. Hesitating long enough to tak
a deep breath, I open the door. Jan stands there beam
ing at me.

"Here we are, right on time and ready to make yo
gorgeous!" Jan announces. She steps into the entry ha
B.J. behind her. Jan looks super, but I stare at B.J. an
wish I could go to the party with a paper bag over m
head. Nobody should razzle-dazzle her good looks lik

B.J. It's unfair to the rest of us who have to live in the same world.

My expression must show what I'm thinking, because the corners of B.J.'s mouth turn up, and she gleams at me. "Stacy, you have great possibilities. With a little makeup and a new hairdo we'll work wonders."

"You should have seen her in the clinic after I did her makeup," Jan says quickly. She holds up an overnight case. "I've got everything here! Even hot rollers and scissors."

"And we'll choose something for you to wear," B.J. adds. "Oh, isn't this fun!"

I take a step backward, bumping into the wall. "Wait a minute. You said to wear jeans. I'm wearing jeans."

They both examine me slowly from head to toe. "They're *new* jeans," B.J. says. "Besides, they're a little baggy. You haven't shrunk them yet, have you?"

"Well, no. I mean, why should I shrink them? They'd be too tight."

"We've got time to shrink them. Take them off."

Jan giggles. "Stacy, you aren't going to wear that flowered cotton shirt?"

"I like this shirt."

Jan puts down her case and opens it. Triumphantly she pulls out a bright red T-shirt with short sleeves and a V-neck. "I brought you a present," she says, handing it to me. "With your dark hair you'll look super in red."

I try to step back again, but there's nowhere to go. "Look," I say, "why can't I just go like I am?"

B.J. tucks her chin down and stares at me with determination. "Because you have something to live up to, Stacy. You're the Sleeping Beauty, coming back to the world, and you have to make an impact on it."

"Don't call me that," I plead.

Jan grabs my hand and pulls me toward my bedroom. "We don't have much time. Let's stop all this talk and get to work!"

They've got a goal, and I'm it. I can't fight the two of them, so I give up and follow orders, getting into a robe as B.J. marches to the laundry room with my jeans and Jan lays out an array of bottles and jars and cans on the bathroom ledge.

She shampoos my hair and plops me into a chair that B.J. has brought from the kitchen. I'm facing away from the mirror over the sink, but that's all right because I'm nervous about what I'll finally see. I just hope Jan knows what she's doing.

Chunks of my hair fall into my lap, and I squeeze my eyes shut. I may need that paper bag after all.

She squirts a handful of some kind of foam into her hands and rubs it all through my hair. Then come the hot rollers.

"So far, so good," Jan says with satisfaction, and B.J. nods approval.

"Now for her face," B.J. says, and reaches for a bottle.

They seem to take turns patting and smoothing things over my skin. Finally I say, "Isn't that enough? This seems like an awful lot of trouble."

"Keep quiet," B.J. says. She picks up a blue pencil. "If you talk, we might make a mistake."

"But—"

"You're going to be our masterpiece," Jan says, and

she giggles with excitement. "Wait till you see yourself, Stacy!"

I can wait. Believe me, I can wait.

"Wait till everybody sees you. Wait till Jeff Clinton sees you!"

"I heard the big exciting news about you and Jeff," B.J. says. From the expression on her face I guess the excitement must have passed her by.

"It's no big deal about Jeff," I tell them. "He just offered to help me learn math. That's all."

"Stop talking," Jan says. "I'm getting to your mouth."

They make enthusiastic comments to each other, which I try to ignore. Finally they step back and grin at me. "Don't look yet," Jan says.

She takes out the rollers, pulls me from the chair, and leads me out of the bathroom back into the bedroom. "Put on your T-shirt before I comb your hair, so your hair won't get all messed up."

"But where are my jeans?"

"Here they are." B.J. comes into the room, holding them out before her. "They're still a little bit warm, but they're dry now."

It takes the three of us to get me into the jeans. I have to lie on the bed and wiggle and grunt and hold my breath until the zipper is up. "I told you they wouldn't fit me!" I complain.

But Jan says, "Of course they fit you. They look just right now. Pretty soon you'll learn how to put them on by yourself. You have to wiggle in just the right way to make it easy."

"You'll get the hang of it," B.J. says, and she helps

me sit up. Stiffly I swing my legs over the edge of the bed. My knees can actually bend. "Good," she says. "Now, don't move until we finish your hair."

As Jan brushes my hair I sneak a quick glance at the clock by my bed. "It's already eight o'clock. We're going to be late."

"Of course we are. Nobody's ever on time," Jan says. "If we get there at eight, they'd think we were nerds."

B.J. sighs. "Stacy, you've got so much to learn!"

Jan steps back. "What do you think?"

B.J. studies my hair, then pokes gently in one spot with the end of the comb. "Perfect," she says, and reaches for the hair spray.

I squeeze my eyes shut as the spray hits my hair, but Jan cries, "Don't ever do that, Stacy! It does terrible things to eye shadow!"

B.J. takes one of my hands, Jan the other. "Come look at yourself," B.J. says. "The Sleeping Beauty emerges."

"Don't call me that!"

But Jan interrupts. "Not the Sleeping Beauty. *My Fair Lady.* That's it. Stacy is like Eliza Doolittle."

"No, I'm *me!*"

By this time I'm in the bathroom. They push me in front of the large mirror over the basin and stand on either side of me. "Well, look!" Jan says.

My hair is shaped so that the front strands barely reach my shoulders, and it's full and wavy and soft. A few tendrils escape over my cheeks and forehead. I reach up automatically to push them back, but Jan grabs my hand. "It's supposed to be that way," she says.

The shadows under my eyes are gone. They're under my cheekbones now, highlighting them. My eyes seem brighter, my lips softer. Jan was right about the red T-shirt. Red is my color. In the T-shirt and jeans I'm snug and straight and so rounded in all the right places that I blush and hunch my shoulders forward a little. B.J. still shines in her own orbit, but now I have nothing to complain about. I won't need that paper bag after all.

I laugh. "Is that really me?"

"Stand up straight," Jan says, and pokes me between my shoulder blades hard enough to make me jerk my shoulders back.

"But I—" My voice drops to a whisper. "I'm so—I mean, on top I—" My face grows even warmer.

"You look just the way you're supposed to," Jan says. She studies me in the mirror. "Don't you like what we've done?"

I have to admit it. "I do. I really do!" I give Jan a quick hug and turn to B.J., but she steps back quickly.

"Don't do that," she says. "Only grandmothers hug."

The telephone rings. Forgetful of everything except the girl in the mirror, the new Stacy, I run to answer.

It's the same voice I heard earlier. The same whisper. "Where are you, Stacy?" it says. "The party's started. We're waiting for you."

This time I slam down the receiver. I'm not going to talk to this jerk. I'm not going to give him the satisfaction of knowing that he's really getting to me. I'm scared at the sound of that horrible whisper. It isn't funny!

I turn around to see B.J. and Jan watching me.

"Is something wrong, Stacy?" Jan asks.

"Somebody I know has a warped sense of humor," I answer. "He thinks he's being funny by trying to scare me."

"What did he say?" Jan asks.

I shrug. "Nothing much. Just whispering about will I be at the party. Real dumb stuff. Second-grade humor."

B.J. and Jan look at each other. "Mort?" Jan asks. "He thinks he's so humorous, and he isn't at all. Remember when he pretended to throw up in Mrs. Watkins's wastepaper basket in front of the whole class?"

"Disgusting," B.J. says, "but I don't think he was invited to this party. At least I hope not."

"Buddy likes to play practical jokes."

"I doubt if it's Buddy."

"It wasn't nice to do to Stacy," Jan says, "and when we find out who it was, we'll totally ignore him."

Each name pops a face into my mind, but I see seventh-grade boys full of mischief, loud belches, and side glances with snickers. Some of them were okay, I guess, but a few were spoiled mean. That was the time of the big oil boom, in which some families in Houston bought bigger houses and guard dogs and handguns and let their fat wallets spill out all over their kids, who grabbed for what they could get and more.

B.J. picks up her handbag. "Let's go," she says.

Their conversation has made me feel better, even though I don't know who they were talking about, so I grab my handbag and follow them to B.J.'s car, making sure a light in the den is left on and the front door is locked.

"You'll have to learn to drive, Stacy," B.J. says. "You can't get around Houston without a car."

"There's a bus to school, isn't there?"

Jan and B.J. give me one of those wide-eyed looks. "We're talking about *after* school, weekends, doing things," B.J. says.

Oh, no. I said the wrong thing again. Embarrassed, I slump against the car seat.

"Sit up, Stacy!" Jan exclaims. "There are a couple of other things you've got to get used to!"

We giggle all the way to the party.

The one-story Maconda house sprawls across an oversize tree-shaded lot that backs onto Buffalo Bayou. Tony opens the ornately carved front door and ushers us into a huge entry hall. Part of my mind takes in the marble and gold and mirrored glass, so that I remember it later, but for the moment I concentrate on Tony. The chubby little boy I knew in seventh grade has changed into someone who is tall with broad shoulders and is very good-looking. He grins at me so appreciatively that I blush.

"Hello, Sleeping Beauty," he says. "You were worth waiting for."

He steps toward me, but B.J. takes his arm, tosses her handbag on a nearby chair, and leads us toward the den. "Come on," she tells him. "We've got to let everybody else meet Stacy."

I follow her into a large wood-paneled den. "Stacy's here," she announces loudly. People crowd around me. Even a woman dressed in a maid's uniform peeks out from the door to the kitchen. I'm overwhelmed by the faces, the voices, the curious stares, the giggles, the questions.

"What was it like, being asleep for so long?"

"How does it feel to be a Sleeping Beauty?"

"Did you have amnesia, Stacy?"

"Do you remember being shot?"

I feel as if I were in a nightmare. The faces are all familiar, yet they're all different. Everyone has changed. I try to match these faces to the faces I remember, and it makes my head hurt.

Suddenly it's more than I can stand. "I don't want to talk about it!"

Jeff has elbowed his way through the group, and he takes my hand. "She means she *can't* talk," he says.

"What do you mean, can't talk?" a girl named Debbie asks. "You make it sound mysterious."

"C'mon, Debbie," Jeff says. "You've seen police shows on TV. You know that nobody's allowed to talk about a case until it goes to trial."

"Oh." Debbie shrugs and looks at me as though I'd suddenly gained a new importance.

A small dark-haired girl in a maid's uniform, who's carrying a bowl of snack mix, pauses for just an instant to stare at me. I hate being a curiosity! I just want to be myself!

I glance around the room. So many faces. Some of them are drifting into groups; some of them are still staring at me. One of the people in this house must be the one who called me, trying to frighten me. How can I look past all those smiles to find out who it was?

"Do you know many of the people here?" Jeff asks.

"No," I answer.

But a stocky guy steps forward. He has brown hair and hazel eyes so light they gleam yellow. He's wearing a linen jacket with the sleeves shoved up. It's almost a twin to Jeff's jacket. For just an instant he glances at Jeff, and I imagine that I feel Jeff's fingers tense. I glance at Jeff, too, but he's standing easily, smile in place.

The stocky guy is staring at me. "Don't you remember me, Stacy?" he asks, and grins.

"No." I shake my head.

He laughs. "Four years make a difference. I'm Jarrod Tucker."

I didn't know Jarrod Tucker well. He was a few years ahead of me in school. He lived down the street from Jan, so I saw him around his house once in a while. Mostly we ignored each other. Jan didn't like him. She said Jarrod was spoiled rotten and bragged that he always got his own way about everything. He's probably changed too. Look at Bick. Four years ago Jan and I thought Bick was sickening, yet across the room she's hanging on his shoulder and looking into his eyes as though he were the most fascinating thing in her life.

"I remember. You lived down the street from Jan."

"Still do," he says.

"But you're a lot older. I mean, this party—you're not—"

He laughs again at my embarrassment. "You're trying to ask why I'm at the party since I'm older than everyone here? Look around. Not everyone. Some of the people who were in high school with me are here too."

"I'm sorry. I didn't mean—"

"Tony and I are good friends," Jarrod adds. "You might say I'm a fixture at most of his parties."

Tony calls out, "Who changed the radio station? All we're getting is commercials." He heads toward the built-in equipment across the room. Jarrod follows him.

A freckle-faced girl edges toward me. "What was it like being out of your head all that time? I mean, did you dream or what?" She looks as spacey as her question.

"No more questions," Jeff says. He murmurs to me, "Let's get you away from the inquisition," and leads me toward a small library. "You need a chance to sit down and relax."

I look around the room. "I like this."

"So do I, and we're lucky. No one else has discovered it yet, so we get a chance to talk."

I sit on the wide sofa that's in front of a wall of bookshelves, and he sits next to me, twisting so that he faces me. I get the peculiar feeling that he's trying to memorize my face.

"Your friends are glad to see you again," he says.

"Are they? I feel like something on exhibit."

"No. It's not like that. Your story is new and different, and they're excited about it."

"But I don't want to be different. I want to go back to school and just be me."

"It will all settle down soon. You'll probably get more questions, but just hang on." He smiles.

"I ought to go home. I feel like I used to when I was a little kid looking on at my big sister's party. I don't belong here."

"It's hard to grow up all of a sudden."

"How do you know that?"

"I can put myself in your shoes. I can imagine."

"Nobody else has tried to do that," I tell him.

"Maybe they just haven't told you."

I shrug. "I don't think so. You're—you're different." I'm furious at myself as I feel my cheeks becoming hot and red. "I'm sorry. I mean— Darn! I sound like a kid. I say all the wrong things."

He laughs as he stands and holds out his hands to me. "You'll learn in a hurry. Come on. Let's get back to the party."

I'm reluctant to join the others. Jeff pulls me to my feet, but I hesitate. Maybe I'm trying to stall. I find myself saying, "I know most of the people in there, but I don't know you. Tell me about yourself."

"There isn't much to tell."

"When did you move to Houston?"

"Around a year ago."

"Where did you live before that?"

"Michigan. Come on, I'm hungry. Aren't you? Somebody said there was going to be pizza."

"Did I know you before, Jeff?"

"I thought you didn't like a lot of questions."

"It's just that I get the feeling that we've met somewhere."

"Where could we have met, Stacy?"

"I don't know."

He heads for the den, pulling me with him. "Maybe I'm just the man of your dreams. Let's check on that pizza."

But as we reach the crowd in the den Jeff and I are

separated, and I see him near the kitchen, talking to B.J.

Jarrod pulls me off to one side and pushes a Styrofoam cup at me. "You've got to be thirsty by this time. Here's something to drink."

I can smell it. Making a face, I hand it back to him. "No way. That's got liquor in it."

He leans close to murmur in my left ear. It tickles. "Come on, Stacy. You're not a kid anymore. This will help you loosen up. You want to have some fun, don't you?"

"Forget it."

"Okay. One soft drink coming up." He squirms a pathway into the kitchen and is soon back with another Styrofoam cup. "Lemon-lime okay?"

Carefully, suspiciously, I smell it, then take a sip. It's all right. "Thanks," I tell him.

I start to move toward the kitchen, but Jarrod says, "The pizzas aren't ready yet. Talk to me." He takes my arm and leads me to a small garden room with floor-to-ceiling glass windows overlooking the backyard and patio with a lighted pool. At the far end of the room a couple has snuggled together in a wicker swing. He's nuzzling her neck. I turn my back on them quickly, blushing again.

Jarrod grins at me. "You really are a Sleeping Beauty, aren't you?"

"Don't call me that!" Angry at him and at myself, I take a long swallow of the soft drink.

"Okay," he says. "You're a beauty anyway." He puts an arm around my shoulders. I stiffen.

"What's the matter?" he asks.

"Nothing," I answer. I'm very much aware of his arm and of the warmth of his hand that is kneading my shoulder. What am I supposed to do? No guy has ever put an arm around me.

"I wonder where Jeff is."

I didn't mean to say it aloud. Jarrod tilts his head to look into my eyes. "You didn't come with Jeff," he says.

"No. I just wondered. I—"

He moves a little closer, and his breath blows warm against my right ear. "It's a pretty night. Want to go outside for a little while?"

The swing creaks, and the girl on the swing giggles. I'd like to get out of this room, so I quickly answer, "Okay. By the pool?" The underwater lights add a glow to the yard that is almost as bright as the lights in this room.

"Better yet," Jarrod says. "Out in front. I've got a new car. I'd like to show it to you."

"Well—"

"Don't you want to see it?" He sounds hurt. "I'm real proud of it. Wire wheels and all sorts of gadgets— even a makeup mirror on the passenger side that lights up. You'll like it. Come on, Stacy." He puts on a little-boy grin. "If you knew me better, you'd know I always get my own way."

I suppose if I had a new car, I'd want to show it off too. "Okay," I say. "I'd really like to see your car."

I look for a place to put down my cup, but Jarrod says, "Drink up first."

I take another long swallow. "That's enough."

"Hey, I got that 'specially for you. Chugalug it."

It's a small cup, and there's not much left. Obediently I take another drink, emptying the cup.

Jarrod takes it from me, grins, and puts it on a nearby table. Holding my hand, he leads me past the couple on the swing, who don't seem to notice us. We go back through the den and the entry hall to the front door. No one seems to notice us. Jarrod quickly opens the door, and as soon as we step through he shuts it behind us.

The night air is still warm, and the light from a large, low-hung moon blurs the dark sky. The sharp, pungent fragrance of early ligustrum blooms is making me dizzy. I find that I have trouble focusing my eyes.

"I feel kind of funny," I tell Jarrod. "I'd better sit down." And I plop onto the top porch step. The bricks are rough and hard.

Jarrod sits next to me. "Get up, Stacy. It's just a few more steps to the street."

"I don't know what's the matter. I'm kind of dizzy. Maybe I'm coming down with a virus. I'd better find Jan."

"Don't bother Jan. You'll be all right. Come on. I'll help you walk."

I try to stand up, but I can't make it. "Let go, Jarrod."

But he doesn't. "Shhh," he says. "Just relax. Just lean against me. Close your eyes, and some of the dizziness will go away."

Maybe he's right. I close my eyes and do feel a little better. As I relax, my head rests against the warm hollow of Jarrod's neck. We sit there quietly for a few minutes. Then he begins stroking my arm with the tips of his fingers, and my skin tingles.

"Feel a little better now?" he murmurs.

"I guess so. I don't know what happened to me."

"You just had a little too much to drink. I didn't know it would hit you this hard, but it won't hurt you."

"What are you talking about? I didn't have anything to drink." It's hard to think. It's hard to figure out what he means.

"Just a little vodka, Stacy. I knew you couldn't taste the vodka."

"Jarrod, you weren't supposed to—" I say, but he interrupts.

"Let's go to the car now," he says.

"No. I think I should go home."

His voice is smooth. "Okay, Stacy. I'll drive you home."

He helps me up. My legs wobble as though the bones weren't connected while we make our way down the three or four brick steps.

As we reach the walkway Tony's front door slams open. Someone leaps down the steps, grabs Jarrod by his collar, and flings him aside. I stagger backward onto the grass and see Jarrod jump up to the top porch step.

"Leave her alone!" Jeff yells.

I stare up at the porch and into Jarrod's eyes.

The screen door bangs against the wall, and I can clearly see the guy who has run from our house. He's scared. I can feel his fear as he stares back at me. His eyes are glittering with terror. They're so light and pale they're almost yellow. I can see his face. He has a gun in his hand. He raises it and points it at me.

"Jarrod!" I scream. "It was you! You killed my mother!"

Chapter Ten

Yelling, screaming with rage, I stagger through a red haze toward Jarrod and directly into Jeff's path as he leaps toward the porch. Jeff and I fall, legs and arms flailing wildly. Jarrod jumps over us and runs to a car that is parked on the drive, facing the street. Jeff stumbles to his feet and races after Jarrod. He slams against the trunk of the car as Jarrod takes off with a screech of tires.

People explode from the house, shouting questions, and I can't stand it. I collapse on the grass, my hands over my head.

"What happened?"

"What's the matter with Stacy?"

"Jarrod? Really? It was Jarrod? I can't believe it!"

"Somebody ought to call the police!"

"Tell them—tell them Jarrod keeps a gun in his car."

"How do you know that?"

"We were on a date. He opened the glove compartment, and I saw—oh, what difference does it make. Someone should tell the police. I don't want anyone to get hurt!"

"Is Stacy all right?"

"Did Jarrod hurt her?"

"Why does Jarrod keep a gun in his car?"

"C'mon. A lot of people do. Tony does."

"Hey, keep me out of this! Anyhow, that's my dad's gun."

"Look, everybody, what should we do about Stacy?"

The questions become a roar, and the words don't make sense. Where is Jeff? Where is Jan?

A hand firmly clasps mine and pulls me to a sitting position. "Open your eyes," Jeff says. "Jan is getting you some coffee."

Jan arrives with a mug of coffee and helps me drink it.

"I hate coffee," I mumble into the cup.

"It doesn't matter," Jeff says. "It will help you wake up."

I can open my eyes now. He's watching me carefully.

"Okay, everybody," Jeff says to the row of white faces with huge, lemurlike eyes. "You can go inside now. I'm going to take Stacy home."

"I'll go too," Jan says.

"You don't need to," Jeff tells her. "She'll be all right."

"But what if Jarrod—"

"The last place he'll come tonight is to Stacy's house."

"Shouldn't we call the police?"

"It's taken care of," he tells them. He turns to me.

"Stacy, is there a particular detective you should talk to?"

"Yes. Detective Markowitz."

"Let's take you home. You can talk to him there. It will give you a chance to calm down."

Jan gives me a questioning look, so I tell her, "I think Jeff is right."

As I watch them leave I mumble to Jeff, "I didn't know what Jarrod was going to do. He wanted me to see his new car." I feel as though I have to explain. "I didn't know about the vodka."

"It's okay, Stacy. You don't have to tell me about it."

"I'm glad you came when you did. Thanks."

"Drink some more coffee."

The coffee has cooled down a little, so I take a big drink. "You came right away."

"I was looking for you. Feeling a little better?"

"Why were you looking for me?"

As I wait for his answer I sip at the coffee. I can think more clearly now, which is unfortunate because I'm getting more and more embarrassed. To make everything worse, I look up at Jeff and hiccup. His face twitches as he tries unsuccessfully to suppress a laugh.

"Home is a good place for you right now," he says. He puts the empty coffee mug on the edge of Tony's front porch. "Come with me, Stacy. My car is across the street."

My legs are working now, but I hold his hand tightly while we walk to the car. In a few minutes, as we pull away from the curb, the nearby streetlight flashes across his face, and again I get the strange feeling that I've met Jeff before.

"You're different," I tell him.

"You said that before."

"I can't explain it. It's like you're not exactly what you seem to be."

He turns to look at me. "You'll find out that many people aren't exactly what they seem to be, Stacy."

"What does that mean?"

"Questions, questions," he says. There's a long pause until he surprises me by asking, "How well did you know Jarrod Tucker?"

"I just saw him around the neighborhood. I knew who he was."

"Did you see him with other people?"

"I don't know. Maybe. I didn't pay any attention. Why?"

"Just asking," he says, but for an instant he gives a strange smile.

"My turn." I sit up straighter. "Do you know Jarrod Tucker?"

He turns and looks at me. "I've seen him around."

"You didn't answer my question."

"Sure I did. Pay attention."

"How come you get to ask all the questions? When I ask you questions, you don't answer or you change the subject."

"Changing the subject right now is a good idea. What do you want to talk about? The party?"

"I don't even want to think about the party." A large hiccup shudders through me, and I clap my hands over my mouth.

The muscles at the corners of his mouth twitch again. He's laughing at me! I open my mouth to tell him that he's rude, but all that comes out is another hiccup. I feel so stupid that I hunch back against the seat and don't try to talk. He doesn't talk to me either. There's such a muddle of feelings stirring inside me. I don't understand them. I sneak a couple of glances at Jeff from the corners of my eyes. I like him. I like to be near him. But there is something about him I don't understand. It's like a secret he doesn't want me to discover.

In a short time we park in the driveway to my house. Jeff leads me up to the front steps, takes the key from my purse, and opens the door. I look at him and gulp. Now what do I do? Will he just say good night? What if he kisses me? I'm terrified that he might, but at the same time I desperately hope that he will.

A rectangle of light suddenly spills from the open front door of the Cooper house, and Mrs. Cooper steps out.

"Is that you, Stacy?"

"Yes, Mrs. Cooper," I call back.

"Your father said you'd be at a party. When I heard a car, I thought I'd check."

"I came home early," I tell her.

"Are you all right?"

"Just tired." I remember my manners. "This is a friend of mine—Jeff Clinton. Jeff, our neighbor, Mrs. Cooper."

They nod at each other, but Mrs. Cooper doesn't go inside. She stands there, watching, as Jeff hands me the key and a scrap of paper.

"My phone number's written on that," he says. "You might want it sometime."

"Thanks," I answer. I wish Mrs. Cooper wouldn't stare at us. "Would you like to come inside?"

From the corners of his eyes he glances at Mrs. Cooper and smiles. "What would your watchdog say about that?"

"I don't care. I—I wish you'd look through the house to make sure no one's there. I'd feel a lot safer."

"No one's there, but if you'll feel better about it, I'll check it out."

I start toward the door with him, but he says, "Stay here. Your watchdog will protect you."

I lean against the rough brick and smile at Mrs. Cooper. "He's checking the house for me," I tell her.

She nods. "Good idea." She still doesn't go inside.

I feel as though I should be making conversation, so I stammer something about what a warm night it is, and she quickly agrees. I'm relieved when Jeff appears in the doorway.

"Everything's okay," he says. "Call Detective Markowitz as soon as you're in the house."

"How did you know his name?"

"You told me."

"I did? Oh. I did. You have a good memory."

"Yes," Jeff says. "I do." Even with Mrs. Cooper watching he leans down and kisses my forehead. "You'll be okay now," he tells me.

As he starts down the walk toward his car I shut the door and lock it, then lean against it, thinking about what a nice guy Jeff is. But why is he such a mysterious person in some ways? He doesn't want to talk about himself. Why? And what did he mean about people not always being what they seem to be?

A thought breaks through the fuzzy fog that has settled on my brain. I realize that Jeff didn't ask me my address. He didn't ask where I lived. But he came here as though he had been here before.

I hear the whispery voice on the phone, the voice that mumbled, "Yes, I have a friend."

What if Jeff is Jarrod's friend?

Detective Markowitz calls me before I can call him. "I got the word on your identification," he says. "They told me that someone at your party phoned it in."

"Yes. I think it was Jeff. A lot of what happened is kind of mixed up in my mind."

There's a pause, and his voice is deeper, quieter. "How about the identification, Stacy? Could that be mixed up too?"

"No. I'm sure. I'm very sure." Then I tell him everything that happened.

"I've got his record in front of me," he says. "Minor stuff. A couple of charges on possession of drugs, but because of his age he was given probation."

"But he's a murderer!"

"That's what we'll have to prove."

"He is! I told you! He is!"

"Take it easy, Stacy. I believe you."

"What are you going to do now? Are you going to try to find Jarrod?"

"There are a number of things to do," he answers.

"I'm working on them. I'll get back to you tomorrow.
You okay?"

"Yes. I'm okay."

"Don't worry about anything. It's up to us for
now."

I remember that Jeff said my house would be the
last place Jarrod would come to, but I can't help asking
Markowitz, "What if Jarrod comes here?"

"He won't," he answers. "Go to bed. Get some
sleep."

"Are you sure?"

"Stacy," he says, and I can tell he's trying to be
patient and is probably tired and wishes he could be
home in bed. "As I told you, I'll get back to you tomorrow."

When I put down the receiver, the house seems
awfully quiet, as if it's listening along with me. I shake
my head. No. I can't frighten myself like this. I'll read a
book. I'll watch something on television. I know what
I'll do. I'll take a shower.

A shower is a perfect idea. The water is hot and
strong. I take a deep breath, then tilt my face up under
the shower head, so that the steamy water beats against
my forehead. When I can't hold my breath any longer, I
twist and duck, letting the force of the water massage
my neck and shoulders. It's warm in here and comfortable, and I wish I could stay here for an hour. But finally
I turn off the water and stretch for a towel that's on the
nearest rack.

The silence in the steam-filled room makes me nervous. I'd forgotten that with the noise of the shower and

the bathroom door closed, I wouldn't be able to hear anything else in the house.

But what would there be to hear?

In the distance the telephone rings.

I fumble with my pajamas and robe, scrambling into them, accidentally turning a sleeve of my robe wrong side out in my haste. I jab at the inside-out sleeve, nearly ripping it as I manage to get it in place so I can pull on the robe.

My hand is on the knob of the bathroom door when I realize that the phone rang only once. That's funny.

Open the door. Don't move. Wait. Listen.

Someone must have known it was a wrong number. Right? Or decided not to call after all. Sure. That's it.

But just to be positive, I cautiously walk through the bedroom hallway. The lights are on in the den, just as I left them. I take another step, and a floorboard makes a snapping sound.

There's a creaking sound in the den, a shadow against the wall, and a voice asks, "Stacy?"

"Daddy?" My voice wobbles. "Is that you?"

He appears at the other end of the hallway. "I thought you heard me come in."

"I didn't. I was in the shower."

"Did I startle you, honey? I didn't mean to."

I run to him and hug him. "It's okay. I didn't expect you to get home so early."

"The reports they sent us were incomplete, so there was no chance to do the work tonight." He turns back to the den, where I see part of an apple on a plate next to his chair. "I was having a snack. There are more apples in the refrigerator. Want to join me?"

"No, thanks." I perch on the end of the sofa. "I thought I heard the telephone."

"You probably did. One of those calls where it dawns on someone that he has the wrong number, but he doesn't say anything and doesn't hang up until he finally figures it out."

"I saw him tonight, Daddy."

"Saw who?"

"The guy who killed Mom. He was at the party. I recognized him."

Dad gives a choking gasp, stumbles toward me, and grabs my shoulders. "What happened? What did you do? Does Detective Markowitz know?"

I hug my father tightly. It makes it easier to tell him about Jarrod and Jeff.

When I finish, Dad drops onto the sofa, next to me. "This Jeff shouldn't have left you alone. He should have stayed with you until I came home."

I'd thought the same thing but found myself defending Jeff. "He said I'd be all right. He did check out the house. Besides, Detective Markowitz told me the same thing."

"Who is Jeff?" Dad asks. "Have I ever met him?"

"Daddy! He just took me home. That's all. He said good night while Mrs. Cooper watched us, and he left."

"Mrs. Cooper?" Dad suddenly looks guilty.

"Did you ask Mrs. Cooper to keep an eye on me?"

"Well, not exactly. The conversation came around to you, and Mrs. Cooper is one of these concerned people, and—" He stops and sighs. "Stacy, I'm doing my best."

"So is Mrs. Cooper!"

Dad laughs, and I have to laugh too. In a way it's funny. "I have to admit, I was kind of glad to see her," I tell him. "I wasn't sure how I was supposed to say good night to Jeff."

"With a firm handshake," Dad says.

"Daddy!"

It's good to hear Dad laugh. It's good to laugh together. But the telephone rings again. Dad reaches for it.

"Hello," he says, and pauses. "Hello? Hello?" He puts down the receiver. "Probably the same idiot."

But I know these aren't just wrong number calls. And I can see in Dad's eyes that what he said was designed to put me at ease. He doesn't believe these are wrong numbers either.

"Are you cold, Stacy? You're shivering."

"I guess I'm just tired," I tell him. "I'd better get to bed."

As soon as the dark seeps through my eyelids I can see Jarrod's face. "I'm not going to let you ruin my life," I whisper to those yellow eyes, "because I'm going to ruin yours!"

Chapter Eleven

Saturday. Long after Dad has left for work, I stretch from strange, troubled dreams into wakefulness. Saturday mornings used to be filled with waking to sun-bright windows and the buttery-sweet fragrance of Mom's pancakes. I almost expect to hear the purr of the lawn mower, which would become a roar as Dad guided it under my bedroom window. Tousle-headed, I'd press my face against the window, squishing my nose, and yell, "You're making too much noise!" Dad—who would follow the game, even though he couldn't hear me over the noise of the mower—would shout back, "Get up! Get up! You've slept away half the morning."

No lawn mower, no pancakes. I make some toast to go with my glass of orange juice. At least there's one Saturday routine I can continue. Today, after breakfast, I'll clean the house.

As I walk into the kitchen the doorbell rings. I freeze, trying to breathe. It rings again. I force myself to shove the fear aside and go to the door. Through the peephole I see a woman standing on the porch. She's well dressed in a denim skirt and pink knit cotton blouse, but her youthful haircut doesn't match the web of tiny wrinkles that stand out under the makeup around her eyes. Beyond her a large black Cadillac is parked at the curb.

I open the door and say, "Hi."

She blinks a couple of times, then raises her chin imperiously. "May I please come in and talk to you?" she asks.

"Why? Who are you?"

"I do apologize. I assumed you would remember." Her stare becomes even cooler. "You're probably having a great deal of trouble remembering people from four years ago—even your neighbors. I am one of your former neighbors."

I still must look blank because she quickly adds, "My name is Eloise Tucker. I'm Jarrod Tucker's mother. I think we need to talk."

I step out onto the porch, shutting the front door behind me. "Could we talk out here?"

"It's warm outside." Her tone is peevish. "You don't have to be afraid of me. I simply want to talk, to clarify a few things."

The porch isn't large enough to have a porch swing on it, so I gesture toward the steps. "I'm sorry, Mrs. Tucker, but—"

She sighs with annoyance and settles on the top step, wrapping her skirt around her legs. I sit on the same step, only as far away from her as possible. She's wearing a perfume that reminds me of dead roses.

She stares at her hands for a moment, then says, "It's about the terrible, unbelievable situation you've

created. About your ridiculous statement that Jarrod
was the person you saw in your house."

"But he was."

"No, dear," she says, "you're wrong because during
that day it all happened, that particular day, Jarrod was
visiting my sister in San Antonio."

"He wasn't."

"My sister and a close friend of hers are going to
testify that he was."

"They'll be lying!"

"It will be your word against theirs. It won't do you
much good to insist on your version.

"As we all see it," she says, "when this tragic inci-
dent happened four years ago, it was a terrible shock to
you. This morning my husband spoke with a noted psychiatrist who feels that it is entirely possible you may
have—well, shall we say, some mental and emotional
problems that are confusing you?"

I lean over, resting my elbows on my legs, clasping
my hands in front of me. "Mrs. Tucker, are you trying to
talk me into changing my mind, or are you threatening
me?"

I suppose I expect her to get angry, but instead, she
calmly says, "To quote our minister, who said he would
be glad to be one of Jarrod's character witnesses, Jarrod
is a willful boy, but he wouldn't shoot anyone."

"He did! He shot my mother. He shot me."

"You saw the gun. Is that right?"

"Yes."

"You had your eyes on it."

"I—I guess so."

"Perhaps you were watching the gun so carefully

hat you didn't really take a good look at the face of the
nan who was holding it."

"But I did!"

"That will be hard to prove."

Now *I* feel like crying, but my tears would come
rom frustration, from rage. "Mrs. Tucker, no matter
vhat you say, I *know* who was on that back porch. I
now who shot me. And I *am* going to testify! Where is
arrod?"

Her tone is sarcastic. "That is what my husband
nd I have been asked repeatedly by the police, thanks
o you. Unfortunately we don't know." She clenches
er fingers so tightly the knuckles look like shiny white
nobs, and her voice lowers and softens as she adds,
'He didn't come home last night."

I lean back against the railing around the edge of
he porch and see, from the corners of my eyes, Mrs.
Cooper busily sweeping her front porch. I pretend not
o notice Mrs. Cooper.

A gray sedan pulls up in front of the house and
)arks behind the Cadillac. The driver's door opens, and
eff climbs out, calling "Hi, Stacy!"

"Jeff!" I jump to my feet.

Mrs. Tucker quickly gets up, leans close to me, and
nurmurs, "Think about what I said."

Jeff's long legs have brought him to the foot of the
)orch steps. He looks at Mrs. Tucker. For an instant I
hink I see a spark of recognition in his eyes before he
)uts on a smile and a bland look and politely says, "Hi."

"This is—" I begin, but Mrs. Tucker, ignoring Jeff,
urries down the walk, jumps into her car, and drives
way.

"You know her?"

"Yeah," Jeff says. "I've seen her around. Jarrod Tucker's mother. Right?"

His smile is open and charming, and I want to believe him. I open the front door and hold it wide. "Would you like to come in?"

"Hello, Stacy!" Mrs. Cooper calls.

I wave back. So does Jeff.

"I'm going to come over in just a few minutes," she says. "I made a tamale pie. All you have to do tonight is just stick it in the oven."

"Thanks, Mrs. Cooper," I call back.

"Shut the door," Jeff says. "We can sit here on the steps."

I settle on the same step, not quite as far away as I had sat from Mrs. Tucker. I wish I had the courage to scoot over close enough so that our bodies would be almost touching. There are all sorts of strange feelings inside me, some of which I like and some which kind of scare me because I don't understand them.

"What did she want?"

"Who?"

"Mrs. Tucker."

"She tried to convince me I had the wrong person. She tried to talk me out of testifying. She even told me that her sister and a friend would testify that Jarrod was with them in San Antonio." I look at Jeff. "Could they do that?"

"Sure. Witnesses can say anything they want."

"But they'd be lying!"

"Some people do lie."

"What if the jury believes them and not me?"

"That can happen."

"Then Jarrod could go free?"

"Yeah. I guess so." Jeff cocks his head as he looks at me. "Instead of asking me all these questions, you ought to ask your Detective Markowitz, who's working this case."

"You're right." I have to smile. "I don't know why I just took it for granted that you'd know."

I pause, and he fills in. "Because I'm obviously wise and highly intelligent and probably know all the answers to everything."

"You're laughing at me."

"No, Stacy. I just tried to cover what you didn't want to say."

"How do you know what I was going to say?"

"Because I have a little brother who's twelve—no, thirteen last month—and he thinks because I'm older than he is I know everything—or ought to know."

I wiggle the toes of my sneakers and watch them intently. I feel so stupid, but in a way I'm glad for what he said. "You told me that you understand. I guess you do."

The telephone rings. I don't care. I like sitting here with Jeff, and I don't want to answer it.

"Get your phone," Jeff tells me.

"It's probably not important."

He jumps up and pulls me to my feet. "On the other hand, it could be. Are you going to answer it, or do you want me to?"

He follows me into the house. I run the last few steps and catch the telephone on the sixth or seventh ring.

"Hello!" I shout. I take a deep breath and try to calm down. "Hello," I repeat, trying to be quiet and dignified.

It's Detective Markowitz. "We picked him up," he says.

"Jarrod? You did? Really? But his mother was just here. Did she know?"

"We're trying to reach his parents. No real urgency, though, since Tucker's an adult."

"What did Jarrod tell you?"

"Nothing," he answers. "I didn't expect him to."

"His mother said her sister and friend would testify that Jarrod was in San Antonio that day. But I know she's lying."

"Oath or not, a lot of people lie, trying to save their own skin or someone else's."

"But I saw him! I'm a witness!"

"I think I told you, Stacy. Placing someone on the scene of the crime is just half of it. We need physical evidence to prove he was there."

"And you don't have any?"

"We may. They did come up with some fingerprints which they couldn't make at the time. We have the casing, which was found in the room, and the slug taken from— Well, at least now that we know what we're going on, there's a slim chance that we might tie Tucker into the scene. To be perfectly honest with you, though, these factors may work out, they may not. That's all I can tell you."

"You also told me about a computer search. What about that?"

"Zilch."

I'm confused and feeling more frustrated by the minute. "What can we do?"

"Come down for a lineup," he answers. "That's as good a place as any to start. It might help us hold Tucker a little longer."

"You mean he might get out?"

"Depends on the judge and what we can come up with to convince him the guy shouldn't be allowed bail."

"I'm going to come to the station right now," I tell him.

"Is anybody there with you?"

"What do you mean?"

"I mean, someone who could drive you?"

"Oh. Yes. A—friend is here. But I'll call my sister and ask her."

As I hang up the receiver Jeff says, "I'll go with you."

"Thanks, Jeff. But I'd better tell Donna where I'm going." I dial her number and give her the latest news.

"I don't know Jeff," she says. "I think your family should be with you. I'll drive you."

"But, Donna—" I don't know how to tell her, with Jeff standing beside me, that I wish she'd butt out for now, that I'd like to be with Jeff.

"I'll be right over," she says firmly, and hangs up.

I turn to Jeff. "She wants to come with me."

"Sure," he says, and smiles. "She's your sister."

He stays until Donna arrives. She smiles and chats, but at the same time she gives him a sharp once-over. Apparently she's satisfied that Jeff is a nice guy because

I can see her relax. She presses a hand to the small of her back and says, "Stacy, we'd better be going."

"I'll be glad to take you there," Jeff says. "It's a good half-hour drive."

I'm hoping she'll agree, but Donna smiles and says, "Thanks anyway, Jeff, but this is going to be a difficult situation. I think it had better be just family."

"Sure," Jeff says. He walks to his car and watches us climb into Donna's. I wish I could turn around and see him drive away.

"He's nice," Donna says.

"I think so too."

I want her to say more about him, but she talks instead about the party and Jarrod Tucker and all the things Dad told her until we reach the police station on Riesner.

As we leave the parking lot Detective Markowitz suddenly comes out from the police building and trots down the steps to meet us. He leads us through a side door. Remembering how busy the lobby was the last time I was here, I'm grateful to miss the crowds.

We enter the homicide room, and he bends to look into my face. "Ready for the lineup?" he asks.

"I'm ready."

He nods, picks up a telephone, punches a couple of buttons, and tells someone to set things up. He puts down the receiver and turns to me. "A few other people will be in the viewing room with us. One of them will be Tucker's attorney. He won't talk to you, but he has the right to be there to make sure everything is done legally, that no one leads you to make a decision. Understand?"

"He has an attorney already?"

"We reached Tucker's father right after we talked to you. The attorney was here within twenty minutes."

I'm glad that Donna is hanging on to me. I don't pay attention to the route we're taking. I can't see anything except Jarrod's face, which has glued itself to my mind.

We're led into a small room. Chairs are facing a glass wall, and beyond the wall is a stage with a height chart made of horizontal lines painted on the yellowed wall behind the stage. Detective Johns is in the room, as are some other men. Donna and I speak to Johns, but no one introduces us to the others. I wonder which one is Jarrod's attorney.

Markowitz tells us to be seated and relax. "The men you'll see out there won't be able to look in at you. This is a one-way glass," he says. "So don't be afraid."

"I'm not afraid."

A door opens at the left. A policeman comes in and picks up a microphone. Then a line of seven men come into the room and file across the stage. Each one is wearing a number on his chest. They all look something alike. "Turn right. Turn left. Face forward," the policeman drawls, as though he'd given these commands so often he could say them in his sleep.

I study the men facing me. I spot Jarrod immediately. His jacket is wrinkled and smudged. He needs a shave. The men with him must have been carefully picked. One of them looks about Jarrod's age, one a little younger. All of them have dark or brown hair. Two of the men are staring at their feet. One has his chin tucked down, throwing his face into shadow.

"Tell them to look this way. Tell them to look at the window," I say to Markowitz. "There's something I want you to see."

Markowitz picks up a receiver and relays my command to the policeman, who barks it out.

The men look upward, to the window that separates us. I look into the pale yellow eyes of the guy who tried to get me away from the party last night. Was it an attempt to get rid of me? If I had gone, would he have succeeded this time in killing me?

What if I identify Jarrod, and he is released on bond? Will he try again? "You won't have a chance," I whisper, as though he could hear me.

Donna is startled. She quickly turns and stares at me. I hear one of the men shuffle his feet. Another coughs.

"Jarrod Tucker is second from the right, and I want you to look at his eyes," I tell Markowitz. "Four years ago those awful yellow cat eyes stared into mine just before Jarrod shot me. I'll never forget his eyes! Never!"

The men in the room look at me sharply, and Donna nervously squeezes my hand. I realize that my hatred for Jarrod has made the room come into focus. I can smell sour body sweat and stale cigarettes, and my tongue curls at the edges with a taste like bitter lemon.

"You're positive?" Markowitz asks. He sounds pleased.

"Merely a formality," one of the men says. "She saw him at the party last night."

I twist toward them. "I'll identify him from photographs," I say eagerly. "Give me his photograph from four years ago, along with others, and I'll pick him out. I promise!"

"Stacy." Detective Markowitz's voice is low as he firmly squeezes my shoulder. It's a signal to be quiet. It doesn't matter. None of them answered me or acted as though they had heard me.

Detective Markowitz speaks to the policeman in the lineup room. In turn, the policeman tells the men to turn around. They file out as they came in, and the door closes behind them.

I stay in my chair, staring into the room. I can still see Jarrod Tucker's yellow eyes.

"That's all for now, Stacy," Detective Markowitz says. "Thanks for coming. We'll be in touch with you."

I stand and look up at him. "How about the gun? Was it in Jarrod's car?"

"We found a gun in the glove compartment."

"And?"

"It wasn't the murder weapon. Different size caliber."

"Oh. I hoped so hard that—" I take a long breath. "Okay. What happens next?"

"Someone in the district attorney's department will want to talk to you, and Tucker will be arraigned."

"Does that mean the trial?"

"No. That means the district attorney will bring a brief summation of the charge against Tucker before a judge, he'll plead not guilty, and his attorney will ask for a trial."

"Then what happens?"

"Among other things, the judge sets the amount of

bail for Tucker or decides if he should be allowed out on bail."

I hear Donna gasp. "You mean he might be set free until his trial?"

"That's a possibility," Markowitz says. "In court we'll present a strong plea that he not be allowed bail, and for now, we can hold him for twenty-four hours without a formal charge."

Donna says, "But even if he's released on bail, surely he won't try to hurt Stacy. He'd have to be insane."

For a moment there's nothing but silence. I know we're all thinking the same thing: *Who says that he's not?*

"Will you let me know what happens to Jarrod?" I ask Markowitz.

"You'll know. You're our witness."

As he talks he moves toward the door. Donna and I follow him out of the room and down the hallway.

Without warning an intense light nearly blinds me, and someone says, "There she is!"

"Don't worry," Markowitz tells us. "It's just a TV crew. They seem to be the only ones who wanted to follow up on the story. The others on the police beat are covering a convenience store shooting on the north side."

Donna is nervous. "What do they want? Can't we get them to go away?"

"I'll chase them off if you say so," he answers, "but Stacy might agree to talk to them for a few minutes. They'll just ask her a couple of questions. They've got word by now on the result of the lineup, and it won't take long. If they ask anything they shouldn't, I'll step in."

"Sure," I say. "It's okay."

A woman with short dark hair is working her way toward me. She's holding up a microphone. The bright light snaps off, so I can see the cameraman with the light and the camera on his shoulder. He's right behind her.

I take a step toward the reporter, ducking around a guy who is being steered through the hallway by a police officer. The guy's face is all scrunched up, as though he were trying not to cry. I don't think he's any older than I am.

Suddenly there's space, and just as suddenly I find myself face-to-face with Jarrod Tucker. He's wedged between two sturdy officers, his hands cuffed in front of him.

His eyes turn to narrow slits as he recognizes me. Detective Markowitz snaps, "Get him out of here!"

Donna tugs at me, the reporter shouts at the cameraman, and I throw up my hands against his instant blast of bright light. Jarrod is jerked past me, the officers with him ordering people to get out of the way, but he manages to twist toward me. Through all the confusion I hear only a snarl of words: "My friend!"

Just as quickly I cry at him, "You're crazy!"

For just an instant, before he's pulled away from me, Jarrod's lips part in a wide grin, and his eyes gleam.

"Donna!" I shriek, but Donna seems to be trying to head off the reporter. Frantically I look for Markowitz, but he has followed Jarrod and the officers down the hall. Nobody's reacting to what Jarrod said to me. Didn't they hear him? Am I the only one?

What did Jarrod mean? That's the second time he's mumbled something about a friend. If Jarrod can't get to me, will one of his friends try?

Markowitz appears at my side. He takes my arm and leads me into a nearby room. "You're shaking," he says. "Sit down." He nudges me toward an ugly chrome and plastic chair.

"I want Donna."

"I'll get her."

I'm alone and more frightened than ever. When Markowitz appears with Donna, I jump up and run to her. I hug her as closely as I can, hanging on as though she were an anchor that would keep me from being swept downstream.

"Don't be afraid," Donna says as she strokes my hair. "Stacy, honey, he's locked up. He can't hurt you."

"He said something about a *friend*. I think he was threatening me. I think he meant his friends would take care of me!"

"He spoke to you?" Markowitz scowls. "I didn't hear him."

"When they took him past me. That's all he said. Just the words *my friend*."

"Are you sure?"

"I'm positive! Don't you believe me?"

Donna speaks first. "There was a lot of noise, a lot of confusion, and you were afraid. Maybe you just thought—"

"The words *my friend*—if that's what you heard— could mean anything, Stacy."

I interrupt them. "I didn't imagine it. I heard Jarrod. I think I know what it means."

Donna wraps her arms around me and says to Markowitz, "There was so much noise, and we were all distracted. It makes sense that Stacy heard him and we couldn't."

"Okay, okay," Markowitz says. He leans against the desk. "I've seen guys like Jarrod Tucker over and over again. They're all brave talk on the outside, cowards on the inside. Threats? Sure, he'd try to scare Stacy out of testifying against him."

"Maybe she shouldn't testify." Donna's chin wobbles, and I know she's close to tears.

I push away from Donna, take a deep breath, and say, "Look, I'm scared. He scared me a lot. But I *am* going to testify against him. Nothing Jarrod can do will scare me out of that!"

Markowitz nods. "We won't let him get to you, Stacy."

"It isn't fair," Donna says, and she suddenly sits on the hard, ugly chair. There are brown smudges under her eyes, and her face looks thin and pale.

"Donna! Are you all right?"

"I'm just tired," she says. "I'm tired of all this. We were a happy family leading normal, average lives. What went wrong? Why should all this happen to us?"

"I'm sorry," Markowitz mumbles, and his eyes do look sorry.

It's not an answer, but for the moment it seems to satisfy Donna. "May I please have a glass of water?" she asks. She sits up a little straighter and rests her hands on her abdomen. Her fingers make a little patting motion, as though she were reassuring the baby.

"Right away," Markowitz says, moving toward the door. But he pauses. "And when you're ready to leave, we'll get you out the back door and away from here. No problem."

"Thank you," Donna says.

But my mind is on Jarrod and the words he whispered at me. He meant to frighten me, and he succeeded. What did he mean? I know what I'm up against with Jarrod. But who is his friend?

Chapter Twelve

On the way back to our house I tell Donna my idea. "I'm going to find out who Jarrod's friends are. As soon as we get home I'm going to call Tony. Jarrod goes to Tony's parties. I bet he'll know."

"It might help," Donna says. Her smile can't cut the worry in her eyes.

But I don't have a chance to call Tony. As Donna parks the car in front of the house, a gray sedan pulls up behind us. Jeff jumps out, lopes over, and opens Donna's door for her.

He walks with us into the house, asking, "Did everything go all right?"

"Yes." For some reason I don't want to talk to him about it.

"Want some iced tea?" I ask him. We follow Donna into the kitchen.

She pulls a large covered pitcher of iced tea out of the refrigerator and hands it to me. Then she pries the lid off a casserole dish and asks, "Why didn't you eat the chicken pasta salad?"

"Because I don't know what it is."

She looks at me oddly. "Oh, Stacy," she says, "I guess none of us did until a couple of years ago."

There's a knock at the back door, and I hear a young voice calling, "Stacy!"

Donna opens the door, and the three Cooper kids tumble inside, each one trying to beat the others in coming out with what they want to say.

"Slow down," I tell them. "Let Teri go first."

Teri quickly shouts, as though the rules might be changed at any minute, "Can we play in your tree house?"

"Oh, no!" Donna says before I can answer. "It's falling apart, girls. It's really dangerous. Dad is going to take it down because it's a hazard."

"I'm glad you asked," I tell them. "You were smart to ask."

"We asked you because when we asked our mother, she said we couldn't," Meri answers.

Keri speaks up. "Can you come over and play, Stacy? We can play dolls again."

I gulp with embarrassment, frantically trying to think of the right thing to say, but Jeff smiles at them and answers for me.

"Not until she baby-sits you again. She'll see you later."

They're out the door like a pack of puppies. I hear them shout their way to their own backyard.

Jeff puts the tips of his fingers against my cheeks. They're cool against my hot skin. "When I was a kid, one of our baby-sitters used to play cars with me by the hour," he says. "I thought she was neat."

"Thanks," I murmur.

"Why don't you stay for dinner, Jeff?" Donna asks. "Dennis will be here soon, and Dad gets home early on Saturday."

"I'd like that," Jeff says. "Mind if I use your phone?"

Donna waves toward the kitchen telephone. Jeff dials and says, "Hi. I'll be here for a while. Okay. Sure." He hangs up.

"In a way I hope the baby is a girl," Donna says. "Girls talk to their mothers."

Jeff laughs. "I'll set the table," he says.

In a moment he and Donna are laughing together, but the telephone call makes me remember. I can't call Tony and ask about Jarrod's friends while Jeff is here. Would Jeff know that much about Jarrod? I can't explain it. I don't want to ask him.

Dad's home on Sunday, and Jan comes over. For some reason Jeff doesn't show up and doesn't call. The maid at Tony's house says the family is at their beach house for the weekend. She'll tell Tony to call me when he gets back, but they might not return until late Sunday night. I keep thinking of Jarrod and wondering why Markowitz doesn't let me know if Jarrod is still in jail or is out on bail. Finally he telephones to say they have a temporary order that will keep Jarrod in jail without bond. A hearing has been set for Tuesday afternoon. There's a lot of talk about the case on the evening news, but all the discussion about possible evidence seems to be rumor. I try all the channels, and no one has any real facts.

Monday morning comes, and Markowitz calls again.

"Regina Latham, one of the assistant district attorneys, is going to work on the Tucker case. She wants to talk to you."

"When?"

"This morning."

"I'll have to call Donna to see if she can take me downtown."

"No need to bother your sister. Just let her know where you'll be. I'll send a car for you. Can you be ready in about twenty minutes?"

"I guess so."

"Okay. I'll meet you there."

"Wait! Don't hang up!"

"What's the matter?"

"I—I don't know what's going to happen. What will she do?"

"Don't worry about that. Mrs. Latham will just go over your story with you, probably ask you a few questions. No big deal."

"Will Jarrod be there?"

"No. Jarrod's locked up tight. Don't worry about him."

I let out the breath I must have been holding. "I'll be ready when your car comes."

True to my word, I'm watching at the window when the car arrives. It's a plain dark brown sedan. I guess I expected a blue-and-white police cruiser. The driver shows me his credentials, and I follow him to the car. It's probably better this way. Another police car might have worried Mrs. Cooper.

But Mrs. Cooper comes out onto her front porch. She calls across to me, "Stacy, is everything all right?"

"Fine," I call back. She looks at the police driver with such suspicion that I add, "I'm being taken to an appointment with one of the district attorneys who's going to talk to me about Jarrod's case."

"Oh," she says, nodding as though there were a spring in her neck. "Well, just call me if you want anything."

"Thanks." I don't want anyone, especially Mrs. Cooper, to keep an eye on me.

The driver opens the car door for me. I climb in and look back as we pull away from the curb. She stands there, watching, until the car is out of sight.

The driver talks about the weather and a lot of dumb stuff like that. Maybe it's a way of killing time. Maybe he's trying to be friendly. Kids don't waste time talking about things that don't mean anything, but adults do it all the time. I suppose that's one more thing I'll have to learn how to do.

We go through the eastern part of downtown Houston, and again I gawk at more new buildings that seem to have popped up as fast as the red tulips Mom used to plant in the front garden each year.

Markowitz meets the car and walks with me into a building where corridors echo with footsteps and voices. An elderly shoeshine man sits just inside the front entrance. "That's the girl," I hear him tell someone as we pass his stand, and I walk a little faster.

As we finally step off the crowded elevator Markowitz says to me, "I'm sorry you have to go through all this, Stacy. It's just part of the game."

"It's not a game!"

He nods. "Sorry again. Wrong word. It's tough for you and for the rest of your family. I know you'd all rather forget it."

His words slap me into awareness. Of course. This whole thing has been horrible for Dad and for Donna. And now they'll have to relive it all again. Blast you, Jarrod! It's not fair!

Markowitz opens a couple of doors, and we're in a small office. Most of the desk and the top of a bookcase are covered with piles and stacks of papers. Behind a clearing in the center of the desk sits a young woman, large glasses rimmed in a tortoiseshell brown that matches her short hair. She's cool and dignified. She stands and, as Markowitz makes the introductions, appraises me.

"The description the press gave her wasn't far off, was it?" she says, and for some reason sounds almost hostile. "Would either of you like coffee? A Coke?" she adds.

Markowitz accepts the coffee, but I don't want anything. I'm too shaky to hold something that might end up in my lap.

"Sit down please, Stacy," Mrs. Latham says, pointing to one of the two chairs in front of the desk. "Just relax." As Markowitz and I sit down she continues. "Now, Stacy, you claim that four years ago you saw someone run out of the back door of your house."

I have to interrupt. "I *did* see someone. And that was Jarrod Tucker."

"Stacy," she says firmly, raising her voice a little like a kindergarten teacher whose students won't quiet

down and get into line, "when this case goes to court—
if it does—"

"What do you mean, *if?*"

Markowitz leans over and puts a big hand on my
arm. "Take it easy, Stacy. Mrs. Latham is an attorney.
She has to make sure that nothing she says can be mis-
construed. Right now she's trying to make sure she's got
a good case. That's all she means."

"Thank you, Detective Markowitz," she says. "I'm
sure that Stacy is old enough to understand the situation."

"I'll try," I answer.

She taps the end of a pencil against the desk and
begins again. "All right. Suppose you tell me in your
own words what you claim to have seen on the day that
your mother was allegedly murdered and you were
shot."

"Allegedly shot," I mutter under my breath. Markowitz coughs loudly, and I wait until he settles back in
his chair. Then I go through the whole story.

Mrs. Latham interrupts me over and over, snapping questions as fast as Jan used to be able to pop
bubble gum. "What exactly did you think you heard?
What kind of sound? Do you recognize the sound of a
gunshot? Have you ever heard one before? Are you
sure you heard anything? Did you know Jarrod Tucker?
Had you ever spoken to him? If you hadn't spoken to
him, if you hadn't been in his classes at school, how is it
you could have been so sure it was Jarrod Tucker on
your back porch? It's been four years since that time.
For that matter could your, uh, illness, let's say, the time

you 'slept,' have affected your judgment or your memory? Maybe both?"

I stand up, slam my hands on the desk, scattering some of her papers to the floor, and explode into tears. "You have to believe me! You're the one who's supposed to make sure Jarrod goes to prison for murder!"

She looks a little frightened by my outburst. "You can't behave like that in court," she stammers.

But Markowitz gently pushes me back into the chair. "She's just a kid," he tells Mrs. Latham.

"She's not many years younger than I am!" Mrs. Latham bristles.

"Don't forget the four years she has to make up for," he answers. He fishes a neatly folded handkerchief out of his pocket and hands it to me. "Stacy, understand that Mrs. Latham is just playing devil's advocate," he says.

"What's that?"

Mrs. Latham looks up at the ceiling as though appealing for help, then back down to me. "It means," she says, "that Jarrod Tucker's defense attorney is going to ask you a great many questions. We're trying to anticipate some of them. We want all the answers *before* we go to court."

I blow my nose and lean toward her, looking her straight in the eyes. "Okay. I want to help in any way I can. But there's a better way to do this. Don't push at me. Don't snap questions at me the way you've been doing it. I came here to work with you, and you're acting like an enemy."

The telephone rings, and she reaches for it so quickly she jostles some papers off her desk. She wasn't the one being rescued. She hands the receiver to Markowitz and says, "It's for you."

His conversation consists of "Good. . . . Clear? . . . Any reaction? . . . I'll check. Thanks." He hands the receiver to Mrs. Latham and nods as though he were in hearty agreement with whoever was on the line. "They did have some clear prints they couldn't make at the time. They check out now. Jarrod Tucker."

"Then you've got physical evidence!" I realize that I'm shouting and jumping up and down in my chair, so I try to calm down. "That means he'll be convicted, right?"

"That means our chances are a whole lot better," Markowitz answers. "A lot of what will happen is up to the judge and the jury and the prosecuting attorney."

We both look at Mrs. Latham.

She sucks in a sharp breath and blinks a couple of times. Finally she says, "Let's start over, Stacy. Maybe I was coming across a little hard and fast. I guess I want to win this case as much as you do."

I sit back in my chair and wait. "Then let's get with it."

"Stacy," she says, and her words are slower, more gentle, "you're very angry at Jarrod Tucker. Are you sure that your emotions are not going to cloud this case?"

"I'm not going to let my anger get in the way."

"How about your resultant feelings of guilt?"

"Guilt? What are you talking about?"

"I mean the common progress in grief. Naturally you'd begin to shift some of the blame from Jarrod Tucker to yourself in cause-and-effect relationships—

for example, your mother's death. If you had been in the house with her, if—"

"No! You're wrong!" I jump to my feet.

She stares at me in bewilderment.

Markowitz stands up. "Mrs. Latham, we've probably covered enough for now, don't you think? I'd like to take Stacy home."

She talks to him as though I were not in the room. "With this emotional instability, I doubt if she'll be a good witness."

"She needs a little time. She'll have it before she has to appear in court."

I take a long breath and force my voice to become steady. "Appear in court as what? I'm only a witness, remember? Or have I suddenly turned into the accused?"

"Stacy—" Markowitz says, but I stand a little taller.

"I'm the victim—on both sides!"

Mrs. Latham slowly rises and says to Markowitz, "Perhaps you can talk to her father. Is she getting any type of therapy?"

"I'll talk to you later," he says, and pulls me out of the office before I can catch my breath and tell her what else is on my mind.

He drives me home in his own car and tries to explain that Mrs. Latham is somewhat new in the department and is trying very hard to prove herself and do things right and that I shouldn't react to everything she said.

"It's going to be a lot tougher than that when Jarrod goes to trial," he tells me. "You'll hear the defense witnesses lie through their teeth, and you'll have to sit there and keep quiet. And Tucker's attorney will blister you with questions, and you'll have to take it."

"Why?"

"Because that's the way the system of justice is set up."

"Justice for whom?"

"Don't be bitter. It's got its flaws, but at least it attempts to give everyone a fair chance."

"Nothing about this seems to be fair. It would have been fair only if somebody had shot Jarrod!"

He doesn't answer. We drive past the Galleria and Neiman-Marcus, and slowly my anger simmers down, like a pot of water with the burners turned off. "Detective Markowitz," I say, "I'm sorry I lost my temper. I acted like a little kid. I won't do it again."

I try to sort out exactly what happened, but one thing puzzles me. "I'll do what Mrs. Latham wants, but she doesn't like me, you know. When I walked in, I could tell that she didn't like me. And I don't know why."

He smiles. "Ummm, could be a little jealousy."

I twist toward him. "Jealousy? About what?"

But he just slowly shakes his head and chuckles. "Stacy, you really are still a little kid."

"You're as bad as she is," I mutter.

"I didn't mean to get you riled," he says. "Let's change the subject."

"Okay. I want to talk about Jarrod's gun."

"I told you. It didn't match the slug and casing we've got on file."

"I know. But when did Jarrod buy this gun? Four years ago he may not have owned one. He might have used someone else's gun—probably one belonging to his father."

He turns to me and smiles. "We're thinking in the same direction. Granted, it's pretty much of a long shot, but we're requesting a search warrant. We can see if Jarrod's father owns any guns, and we can subpoena them for testing. The Houston Police Department has one of the best ballistics experts in the United States. If there is anything to be found out, he'll find it."

"Before the hearing?"

"It doesn't have to be before the hearing."

"I want to be there."

"Have anyone to take you?"

"I'll ask Donna."

He's silent for a minute, and I know he's thinking of what Donna went through in the police station. "Let's leave your sister out of this. I'll send a car for you. The driver will be at your house around two."

"Thanks."

"It's okay. Now, do me a favor and relax."

I lean back against the seat and try to relax. I really do. Especially I try not to think of everything Mrs. Latham said.

But when I'm finally in the quiet, lonely house, it comes back to me. I pick up the picture of Mom that Dad keeps on the dresser in their bedroom. She's squinting against the sunlight and laughing as though someone had just told her a wonderful joke.

"Oh, Mom, it wasn't my fault, was it?" I ask the picture. The picture just smiles back. I sit on the floor, my back against their bed, hugging the picture to my chest. For the first time I wish I could cry. But the tears are locked behind the hard lump of hatred that grows and chokes and burns inside me. I can't get rid of that hatred, and nothing can help me get rid of it. Not until Jarrod is dead!

Chapter Thirteen

Early Tuesday morning Jan calls to invite me to dinner. I promise to come over to her house around five. As soon as Jan is off the phone I call the head counselor at the high school. I find out his name is Mr. Dobbis.

"Oh, we're right up on our toes about your case," he says, and I picture him pirouetting around his office in toe dancer shoes. "Come to the office now if you'd like to," he adds. "We were going to give you a little more time, but I've already met with your seventh-grade teachers, and gone over your records, and have a pretty good handle on a plan for your future studies."

"Will I have to go back to middle school?"

"No. Come on, and we'll talk about what I have in mind."

Dad gives me a lift to the school and shows me a bus stop where I'll be able to catch a bus that comes down Memorial Drive. From there I can walk home.

"Remember, I'll be at Jan's house for dinner tonight," I tell him. "She'll bring me home—probably around ten."

"Then I won't come home for dinner," he says.

"Don't work too hard, Dad."

He just smiles, waves, and drives off.

The high school is a mixture of old brick and modern, with two-story buildings stretching across a large campus. There are lots of trees and a wide grass lawn in front of the school. At the side is a gigantic parking lot. Kids are beginning to arrive for classes, and the street in front of the school is almost blocked with a chain of cars trying to get into the parking lot. I keep swallowing as I go up the steps of what looks like the main building. I have to ask a second time how to find Mr. Dobbis's office, because I'm so nervous I can't remember what the first person told me.

I'm in Mr. Dobbis's office for about an hour, talking about makeup study and exams and the school's tutoring program and summer school, and I leave feeling pretty good. It's going to mean a lot of work, but I can do it. He thinks I can, and I know I can. There's no way I can graduate with my class, but I honestly didn't expect to. With math and science and four years of English and everything I'll have to cram in, I couldn't cover it that fast. But at least it won't take four or five years. I won't be the oldest student in the history of the world ever to graduate from high school.

I smile to myself as I leave his office, hugging the books he gave me, and plunge out into the hall. It's filled with fast-moving bodies, and I find myself pushed aside. I plaster myself as flat as I can against the wall, trying to stay out of the way.

Someone skids to a stop in front of me. "Stacy?" Tony asks. "What are you doing here?"

"Tony! You didn't answer my phone call."

"Yeah. Hey, well, I was busy." He begins to move off. "I'll see you."

"Don't go." I grab his arm.

"Look, I'll call you tonight."

"What I have to ask you won't take very long. You're one of Jarrod's friends. Right?"

The pupils of his eyes flick to each side, and he licks his lips. "Not really friends. He comes to my parties, if you know what I mean."

"No, I don't."

"You're really dense."

It takes just a moment for what he said about Jarrod to sink in. I tighten my grip on Tony's arm as I say, "You're telling me he has a reason for being at your parties. Are you talking about drugs?"

"I gotta get to class, Stacy. Let go."

"Answer my questions, or I'll start yelling and screaming."

Again he seems to check from side to side, then leans close. "So he's a supplier. Most of the kids know it."

"Why hasn't he been arrested?"

"Proving it is something else." He scowls at me. "And don't go telling your cop friends."

Friends. "One more question. Who are Jarrod's friends?"

"A guy like Jarrod doesn't have friends."

"You must have seen him with someone."

He thinks a minute. "Yeah. Sometimes he comes on the grounds here. Sometimes I've seen him at places he hangs out. I've seen Jeff with him. Remember Jeff Clin-

on? He was at my party. Somebody said he took you
ome."

I clutch my books to my chest and shiver, but a big
guy barges into Tony, knocking him off-balance, so he
doesn't notice. "I gotta go, Stacy!" he complains.

A bell rings. The hall is emptying fast. "Go ahead,
Tony. Thanks for answering my questions."

"Remember," he says, "keep some of that information to yourself."

I have to lean against the wall for a few minutes.
The metal locker is cold, and the handle pokes into my
back. But it doesn't seem to matter. Everything seems
to be all wrong. Tony must have been lying about Jarrod's friend. It couldn't be Jeff.

I find myself walking down the hallway toward the
main doors. I've got to go home.

As I walk into the house, about forty minutes later,
the telephone rings. I don't want to answer it, but what
if it's Donna? What if it's Dad? So I clutch the receiver
and manage to say a weak "Hello?"

It's Detective Markowitz. "Mrs. Latham has some
more questions she wants to go over with you," he says.
"Do you feel up to it?"

"Now?"

"As soon as we can get you downtown. She wants to
get more information from you before the hearing.
There are some things you didn't cover in your first
meeting."

"Okay."

He pauses. "Uh, Stacy, she's kind of unbending, but

she's a good prosecutor. If you could relax with her—
The sentence dangles.

"I'll stay calm," I promise him.

"Fine."

"Do I have to testify at this hearing?"

"No. It's just to set a date for Tucker's trial, give hi
attorneys a chance to ask for a postponement, all tha
sort of legal stuff. You don't even need to be there."

"But I want to be there."

"Believe me, it won't interest you."

"Yes, it will. Really."

"Get ready," he says. "The car will be at your hous
in about twenty minutes."

I change from my jeans and blouse to a dress.
want to look just right. If I had a suit, I'd wear that. I ca
be just as businesslike as Mrs. Latham.

The driver from HPD arrives. I wave to Mr
Cooper, who comes out on her porch again. How ca
she be so aware of everything that's going on?

She calls to me as I'm climbing in the police ca
"Stacy, it's all right about that car."

The driver shuts the door, so I roll down the wir
dow and stick my head out. "What car?"

"Tell you later," she yells.

We soon arrive at the courthouse, and again it's
quick hello to Detective Markowitz, through the lobb
with him, into the elevator and up to Mrs. Latham
office.

She's a little less formal with me now, and I don
let her officiousness get to me. If she's a superprosecu
tor, then that's what I want. For some reason she slow
down on the questions, so I don't feel bombarded, and

answer them over and over and go into all the details I can remember.

It doesn't take long. She looks at her watch and says, "Very good. I think I have all the information I'll need for now. I'll go to court and see what I can accomplish."

"I'm going to be at the hearing too."

Mrs. Latham looks at Markowitz, who just shrugs. "Some of the media will be bound to be on hand," she says.

"I thought they had written enough about it," I say. "It hasn't been on TV or in the newspapers lately."

"It will again. They'll cover each new development."

"I don't care. I have to be there." I can't explain to either of them that I need to know what is happening each step of the way, that I need to *see* Jarrod standing before the judge.

We go to another floor, where each door along the hallway opens to a courtroom. Mrs. Latham leaves us, and Markowitz and I enter one of the courtrooms, and slip into seats near the door in the third row. The room is painted a shade of off-white, and the seats are like padded theater seats. A large desk faces us at the far end of the room, and I know that's the judge's bench. Flags of Texas and the United States hang at one side of his bench. There are no windows in the room. I feel closed in, a little panicky, but I won't leave. I huddle against the curved, molded back of the seat and hug my elbows for comfort.

A well-dressed woman enters the room, pauses for just a moment, and glares at me. It's Mrs. Tucker. A man joins her. She murmurs something to him, nodding in my direction. He gives me an angry glance, then ushers her into one of the seats at the opposite side of the room.

A woman bustles back and forth between the judge's bench and her desk. A few other people are in the room, and more straggle in. Four men carrying briefcases push their way through the hinged panel that separates the front section of the courtroom from the seats for visitors. They chat as though they were friends, then separate, going to opposite ends of a long table in front of the judge's bench. Mrs. Latham arrives and begins to talk to a couple of the men. They both look up at me, then go back to their conversation.

"I told you, this will be boring," Markowitz mumbles.

I just shake my head. He doesn't understand how much I need to see this happen.

"Everything going all right for you?" he asks, so I tell him what Tony had said about Jarrod and drugs.

He doesn't seem surprised. He just says, "That won't figure into this case."

"But it shows what kind of person Jarrod is!"

"The trial will be concerned with whether or not Jarrod Tucker was the person who murdered your mother. Whether or not he's supplying drugs now has nothing to do with what happened four years ago."

"You mean, he's going to just get away with the drugs thing?"

"I didn't say that. We have a narcotics department. I can pass along what you told me and let them look into it."

"You should work together."

He stretches out his long legs. "We do work together."

"Well, I think—"

I don't have time to tell him what I think because the woman near the judge's bench suddenly announces the arrival of the judge, and we all stand. A tall gray-haired man strides in, his black robes billowing around him. He sits down, and everyone in the courtroom sits down too.

A door at the far end of the room opens, and two men dressed in tan uniforms come through. A young man in jeans and what looks like a jogging shirt is between them.

"Who are they?"

"Bailiffs," Markowitz whispers, "with one of the prisoners."

"But where's Jarrod?"

"On the other side of that door is a holding pen, where prisoners are kept until it's their turn to see the judge or to be taken back to jail."

One of the prosecuting attorneys quickly goes through charges against the man before the judge. His attorney says something to the judge about the man's lack of a previous record, and the judge sets bail of $5,000. The attorneys go over to talk to the court clerk. Everyone on the judge's side of the railing seems to be talking, but I can't hear what they're saying. In a few minutes the bailiffs go off with the man, and another one comes in with an elderly woman who looks like a bag lady.

"When will they bring in Jarrod?"

"Be patient. I told you this would be boring."

Finally the first two bailiffs return. They enter the courtroom with Jarrod walking between them. He's dressed in a really sharp suit, white shirt, and tie. He looks like a model student here to accept an award. They stop at the right end of the table. The two men who have been sitting there stand and talk to Jarrod. I recognize one of them. He was there at the lineup. Jarrod's attorney. I can't hear what they're saying. They point to a chair between them.

Jarrod's mother makes a little whimpering noise, and Jarrod shifts to look at her. His lower lip curls downward, and he looks like a spoiled little boy ready to throw a tantrum. I think Jarrod hasn't noticed me, but before he sits down, he turns and stares at me. One corner of his mouth twists, and he glares with such fierceness I gasp. I get his message. I couldn't miss it. But I know it as well as he does. Without my testimony there would be little way that Jarrod could be convicted of murder. I know Jarrod would like to kill me if he could only get the chance.

Markowitz seems to know what I'm thinking. He puts a hand on my arm. "Don't worry about him," he says. "He's under guard. There's no way he could get to you."

"I'm not afraid," I whisper. But I am. A little. Even though Jarrod's back is to me, I keep seeing his pale yellow eyes, surprised and horrified as we face each other in our backyard. And I see the gun.

Maybe I'd be more afraid if I didn't hate Jarrod so much. Markowitz and Mrs. Latham might think I want to be here because I'm curious. They couldn't know about the hatred that burns and hurts and makes me want Jarrod to be punished for what he did.

I can't quite follow everything that goes on. I do hear Jarrod's attorney claim that Jarrod has been arrested four times on charges of possession of drugs, he's been given probation in all cases, and he has no record of violence. The attorney asks that Jarrod be released without bail. I want to jump up and yell at the attorney, but Mrs. Latham is talking to the judge, and the judge gives these little nods as if he were keeping time. I hope he's agreeing with her.

But suddenly Jarrod flings himself up, twists, and groans. All the people in the court stare at him like openmouthed statues. He shudders and makes a horrible, retching noise, drops facedown on the floor with a loud plop, twitches, and is still.

Jarrod's mother screams, runs to him, and kneels next to him. "What did you do to him?" she shouts.

The bailiffs have sprung to life. One of them crouches next to Jarrod. The other tries to pull his mother back. The first bailiff calls out to the judge, "He's out cold, but he's breathing. It's not very regular. We'd better get an ambulance."

The judge has stepped down from the dais and is walking toward Jarrod. "It looked like some kind of seizure." He looks at Jarrod's parents. Mr. Tucker has joined his wife and has an arm around her shoulders. "Does he have some kind of medical history we should know about?"

But Mrs. Tucker isn't coherent. She cries and accuses, and a lot of what she's saying is muffled against her husband's chest. Mr. Tucker looks as though he were going to be the next one to pass out.

"He's got a good pulse," the bailiff says.

"Paramedics are on their way," one of the clerks calls to the judge.

The judge gives a final nod at Jarrod, who lies there without moving, and strides back to the bench, his robes billowing behind him like black sails.

After he's seated, he states, "When Mr. Tucker has recovered, we'll set another date for a hearing. For now he'll be taken to the Ben Taub emergency room and kept under guard."

A jabber of noise from the hallway bursts through the door with two paramedics. They run to Jarrod and begin their work. Someone in uniform secures the door.

"Let's go, Stacy. We're in the way here." Markowitz pushes out of his seat, and I follow him.

In the hallway we're met with blinding lights from television cameras. Microphones are shoved in my face. I recognize Brandi Mayer among some other reporters with notepads and tape recorders. They surge at me, asking questions that confuse me.

"Do you still think Jarrod Tucker is the one you saw four years ago?"

"Have you had amnesia?"

"Are you seeing a psychiatrist?"

"How do you feel about those lost four years?"

"How do you feel about Jarrod Tucker?"

I don't know how to answer. I just want to stand still and scream. But Markowitz fields for me, edging through the crowd, tugging me with him, answering some of the questions for me, until an elevator arrives and we can escape inside.

"There will be a lot of this," he says. "Better get used to it."

I lean against the back of the elevator. "In the beginning I thought you'd just arrest Jarrod, and there would be a trial, and it would be over."

The elevator doors open, and he quickly leads me down a back hallway to the parking lot and into his car. When we're out on the street, he finally answers. "There's a lot more to it than that. There will be a trial, but if the verdict goes against Jarrod, his attorney will automatically appeal it, and you'll have to testify again. I've seen his attorney operate before. Unfortunately he really knows how to badger witnesses. Just be prepared for him—and for the press. They'll be interested in you and your family until all this is over."

"My family? But Dad and Donna shouldn't be a part of this!"

"To the media they are."

"Why do they ask so many questions?"

"It's their job."

"But it's not fair!"

"Get used to it, Stacy."

As I climb into the car I glance back at the courthouse. None of this would be happening if Jarrod Tucker were dead. With all my heart I wish he were dead!

Soon after Markowitz has taken me home, Jeff arrives. When I open the door, he says, "Your next-door neighbor just came out on her porch. Shall we sit out on the porch or ignore her?"

Before I can answer, he says, "Let's ignore her. It's hot and I'd like a Coke." He steps in and closes the door. I hear the latch click as the dead bolt turns.

Maybe I look startled, maybe a little scared because Jeff says, "Have to be careful."

He leads the way to the kitchen, and I follow him. It occurs to me, as I put the Cokes on the kitchen table and sit opposite Jeff, that I could run over to Mrs. Cooper's. Or I could tell Jeff what Tony said about him. I don't do anything but watch Jeff and sip at the icy drink.

Jeff raises his head to take a long swallow from the can, and I watch the muscles work in his throat. I'd like to reach out and touch his throat. I'd like to be close to him, to feel his arms around me. I'd love to have him kiss me. I've never felt like this about anyone before. I try to explore my mixed-up feelings, but they don't make any sense.

Jeff puts down the can and tilts his chair back. "You had a rough time at the courthouse."

Suddenly I'm cold. "How did you know what happened at the courthouse?"

"It was on the television newscast," he answers easily.

From where I sit I can see the kitchen clock. "The first newscast won't be on for half an hour."

"Must have been on the radio, then," he says. "I know I heard it someplace."

Jeff is lying. I can tell. Why would he lie to me?

"I heard that you went to the high school this

morning to talk to the head counselor," Jeff says, quickly changing the subject. "Did you get things straightened out?"

Carefully I answer, "For the most part. Making up all that work won't be too bad."

"I hope you still want a tutor."

My voice is so low I wonder if he can hear me. "Yes, I do."

His expression changes. The smile slips, and his eyes become serious. "Tony said you had a lot of questions to ask him."

I can't answer. I don't know what to say.

Jeff leans across the table and takes my left hand. I hope he can't feel it tremble. "Stacy," he says, "don't believe everything Tony might have told you." His eyes look kind of strange, almost sad, as he adds, "Don't believe in anybody but yourself."

Chapter Fourteen

The telephone rings, and I snatch it, grateful for the interruption. It's Brandi. She asks if I'd mind just a couple of questions.

"I'm sorry," I say. "Not now. I—I'm sorry."

As soon as I hang up, the phone rings again. It's another reporter—this one calling long distance from a newsmagazine.

"No," I say. "Not now!"

It rings again, and I just stare at it, shaking my head. "I don't want to talk to reporters," I tell Jeff.

"You don't have to," Jeff says. He puts a hand on my shoulder. He's standing very close to me. "Don't be afraid, Stacy," he murmurs.

How can I tell him that he's the one I'm afraid of?

The doorbell chimes insistently.

Jeff is ahead of me as I hurry to the door. He opens it, but Mrs. Cooper twists around him to thrust a steaming loaf of bread at me.

"Take the potholders too!" she exclaims. "The bread is right out of the oven, and I don't want you to burn your fingers."

I remember my manners. "Would you like to come in?"

Instead of answering, she smiles at Jeff and says, "I thought I'd just stop by for a visit."

"I'm sorry," I tell her. "I'm going to my friend Jan's house for dinner. I'll be leaving here in a few minutes."

"I've got to go too," Jeff says. "Lots of homework. See you later." As he reaches the walk he turns and adds, "Both of you."

Mrs. Cooper seems greatly relieved. "It's just as well. I've got to get home. Dinner to make, you know." She smiles lovingly at the loaf of bread I'm holding. "It's too bad you can't eat that with your dinner, Stacy."

"I'll love it for breakfast," I answer.

She watches Jeff drive off, then says, "Oh, yes—about that car. It's all right."

"I don't understand what you mean."

"The car I told you I saw driving around and around this neighborhood. I've seen it again, but with one thing and another I just didn't mention it to you, but there it was, and—"

I shouldn't interrupt, but I can't stand it. "What about the car, Mrs. Cooper?"

"It's his," she says, and looks pleased with herself.

It takes a moment to register. "It was Jeff's car you saw?"

"Yes," she says. "So it's all right. Enjoy the bread." She's off on a trot to her own house.

I carry the bread to the kitchen. It's yeasty and buttery, and I'm hungry, but I've got something more important to think about than a loaf of bread. Why would Jeff—I can't put the question into words. I'm afraid of the answer.

Our telephone rings again. Automatically I pick up the receiver, and a deep voice begins telling me he's with one of the Houston television stations, and how do I feel about testifying against Jarrod Tucker?

"What do you mean, how do I feel?" I stammer. "I want to testify!"

"You're not afraid of him?"

"Jarrod's in jail."

"For how long?" the reporter asks. "Even if he goes to trial and gets a life sentence, he can be paroled in twenty years—twelve, if he gets time taken off for good behavior."

"That can't be true."

"It's true. Check it out. How does your family feel about your decision to testify?"

"I—I don't know. I don't want to talk to you anymore!"

The moment I put down the receiver the telephone rings again. I won't answer. Those reporters will have to give up sooner or later. I don't want to talk to them. I have to think.

I curl up in Dad's recliner with an apple, taking big, angry bites out of it as I try to sort things out. What's happening is like a nightmare, but it's not something that will go away when I open my eyes. And it's not like the stories I read and the Saturday-morning cartoons I watched when I was a child. The bad guys aren't caught and carried away so that the good guys can live happily ever after. Maybe a jury will give Jarrod the death penalty. Maybe it won't. How long am I going to have to live with fear of this man who has already robbed so much of my life? And it's not just me! What is all this going to do to Dad? And to Donna and Dennis and their baby?

If I had the chance, I would kill Jarrod Tucker.

At first the thought startles me, and I push it away. But it comes back, and I examine it, turning it over in my mind, testing the sharpness of its edges, feeling the hatred that makes it strong.

The phone has stopped ringing, and the silence of the house settles around my shoulders. Late shadows fade the colors of the room like a coating of dust. I should have been at Jan's house an hour ago. I'd better hurry and get ready.

I'm suddenly uncomfortable with the silence because through it pop and creak the settling sounds that houses make. I turn on the television, not listening to words, just wanting noise to blot out the quiet.

The doorbell chimes again, but this time I don't answer it. I peek through the curtains at the front window to see who is on the porch. Mrs. Cooper. She's the last person I want to talk to right now.

She gives up and leaves the porch. She cuts across the lawn to her house. A marked police car cruises around the corner and slows down as it passes our house. Did Detective Markowitz arrange for this? I step back from the window, but not before I see the police car pull to a stop while Mrs. Cooper runs down her walk to talk to the officers. Does she have to know about everything that is going on? The car moves on, and Mrs. Cooper heads back to her house.

Jan is going to wonder why I'm so late. I'm in the

den, on my way from the living room to the bedroom to get my handbag, when I hear a slight rattling noise close at hand. It seems to be coming from the side door that leads to the garage. I stand and listen, waiting for the sound again, but it's the words on the television that I hear.

The announcer is saying, "In an escape while being examined in Ben Taub Hospital a short while ago. A bailiff was shot in the leg when his gun was taken by Tucker. An HPD spokesman told us that an all-points bulletin has been put out for Tucker, who is believed to have stolen a dark blue Pontiac and is thought to be heading out of state, possibly toward Louisiana."

The noise from the hall door that leads to the garage rattles over the announcer's words, and I see the doorknob turn.

I know who's at that door. It has to be Jarrod. He's inside the garage, and soon he'll be inside our house! No one would suspect that he'd come here. He'd have to be crazy. But didn't he warn me he always gets his own way?

For an instant I freeze, unable to move, desperately wondering what I can do. I have to pass the door leading to the garage to get to the front door. Jarrod will have that door open in a minute. I'll run right into him. I can't hide in the house. He'll find me. If I can make the backyard—

As quickly and quietly as possible I move to the back door and open it carefully, wincing at the slight sounds it makes. I shut it and run into the yard. Now what?

I hear one of the Cooper children complaining

about having to come in; then the Cooper back door slams. I take two steps in that direction when I realize I can't endanger their lives. This is between Jarrod and me.

In front of me is the oak tree and the nailed board steps that lead up to the tree house. Jarrod won't look for me there.

I scramble upward, clinging to the trunk and branches. My foot slips as one of the boards tears loose from the tree, and I skin my elbow. I'm so scared it's hard to breathe, and my fingers feel like numb stumps as I pull myself up and drop to the floor of the tree house. Frantically I tuck my legs inside and shove myself against the back wall.

But the tree house rocks unsteadily. I hear a board from it drop to the grass. I inch to the center and sit perfectly still. Miraculously the house steadies itself. My back is against a window, but the window is on the Cooper side and shielded by a large branch. If Jarrod comes outside—and I don't think he will—he won't be able to see me through this window. I wait. There is nothing I can do but wait.

Forever is measured not in minutes but in heartbeats. I can hear the steady thumping pulse in my ears. Shadows are deeper, but time has dissolved into terror.

Then I hear what I've been dreading. The back door to my house opens and shuts. Jarrod is in the yard.

"Stacy?" He mumbles something after that, but again, as on the phone—for now I'm sure it was him—it's as though he were talking to himself.

The voice comes from below me, as soft and shivery as the warm night breeze from the Gulf. I try not to move. Can he hear my trembling?

He chuckles, and the sound is even more fearful than his voice. "You've got to be up there," he says.

Instinctively I shrink back even farther. The boards in the tree house groan loudly, and it rocks.

"I could shoot you from down here," I hear him say. "But I don't want to shoot you. I want you to have an accident." He laughs to himself again.

I hear the sound of his shoes scraping the trunk of the tree as he climbs toward me. "Stacy," he says, "I told you—I always get my own way."

Suddenly a calm sweeps through my mind, and I stop shaking. I am not going to sit here and wait for Jarrod to have his own way. I'm a woman who's able to think rationally, to want *my* own way. And I have a plan.

Slowly, careful to keep the tree house balanced, I slide upward, grasping first the rough edges of the window behind me, then reaching for the branch outside it. I have managed to pull myself out the window, with my feet resting against the lower window frame, by the time Jarrod's arms and grinning face shove into the door to the tree house.

I stare into his yellow eyes. I see the gun.

"If I'm killed, they'll know you did it!" I whisper.

"Not if it's an 'accident.'"

"You're insane!"

He giggles. "Smart girl, Stacy," he says. "I've set it up. That's going to be my defense. Now, let's talk about your 'accident.' My friend and I will take care of it."

"Your friend?"

"This is my friend." For just an instant he takes his eyes from me as he gives a little wave of the gun in his hand.

As hard as I can I kick against the side of the house, swinging into it, throwing all my weight against it.

The house, with a great groan and crash, collapses and falls, taking Jarrod with it.

I scramble down and drop from the tree, into his screams and curses. Jarrod is lying on his back. Some of the boards are under him, and the large part of the tree house covers his hips and legs.

The gun lies near my feet.

I pick it up, hold it carefully in my right hand, and slip my index finger against the trigger.

Jarrod has stopped yelling. He stares at me. I can see the back door of our house fly open. I can see the terror on Jarrod's face, the gleam in his eyes. I can see his gun pointing at me.

"Don't shoot me," Jarrod whimpers, and I realize I am pointing the gun at him.

If I shot Jarrod, wouldn't it be self-defense? And wouldn't it end the trials and the questions and the badgering and the harassment and the nightmares and the worries and the years and years of fear?

Carefully I aim the gun.

Chapter Fifteen

"You can't shoot me!" Jarrod is crying and slobbering. Spittle drools from his mouth and down his chin. Or is it blood? "I didn't mean to kill your mother. I didn't know she was in the house, but she came into the den from the kitchen, and saw me, and said something to me, and I was scared. I didn't mean it, Stacy!"

I try to picture my mother facing Jarrod with his gun. "What did she say to you?"

"She didn't say anything at first. She was smiling. Then she saw the gun, and her eyes got frightened, but she still had a kind of smile on her face. She held her hands toward me and said, 'It's all right. It's all right.' "

"And you shot her!"

He can't talk. He's crying too hard. I aim the gun at his head, just as carefully as he once aimed it at me. My hands have stopped shaking.

But now I can picture my mother. I can see her smile too. I can hear her telling Jarrod, "It's all right." Tears rush to my eyes with such force I'm blinded. I try to rub them away with the back of my left hand.

Choices were so easy when I was a child. Good guy

versus bad guy, and the good guys always won. But I'm no longer a child.

Although I keep the gun pointed at Jarrod, at the top of my lungs I yell, "Help! Mrs. Cooper! Help!"

I hear her scream, "They're coming! I already called the police!"

"I'm all right," I shout to her. "Don't be afraid. I'll keep the gun on him until the police get here."

Someone leaps the hedge and lands beside me, but it isn't Mrs. Cooper.

"Give me the gun, Stacy," Jeff says.

"No!" I don't take my eyes off Jarrod. "Stay away from me. Mrs. Cooper called the police. They're coming."

"I *am* the police. Narcotics squad," he says. "You can give me the gun."

He reaches across and takes it out of my hand.

"My leg's broken!" Jarrod begins to yell again. "She did it. She tried to kill me!"

I look up at Jeff. "How can you be a policeman? You're just a senior in high school."

But, as always, he avoids my questions. He even sounds a little angry. He keeps his eyes on Jarrod. "You could have been killed, Stacy. Apparently you were home and weren't answering the phone. Why not?"

Jarrod groans. "My back. It hurts. I think something's busted. Get an ambulance!"

"It's on its way," Jeff tells him.

"Jeff, I had Jarrod's gun. I could have shot him."

He doesn't look at me. "Could you?"

I shake my head. "No. Not really. I wanted to. I

hated him so much that I really wanted to kill him. I almost did. But then I couldn't do it. Mom wouldn't—"

It's hard to explain. I hope that Jeff understands what I mean. I add, "I really didn't have a choice. Jarrod's life doesn't belong to me." I think of all the problems to come for all of us because of Jarrod, and I give a long sigh.

The yard seems to be filled with people. Mrs. Cooper is talking at a great rate. To me? I hear the high, excited chirps she's making, but the words don't come through. There's a bass note in my ear as an officer with a notebook peers at me, asking me questions. But the only words I want to hear are Jeff's.

He has my arm, propelling me around the rubble and the police officers, through our back door and into the house. The familiar, dusty smells of the room are laced with the pungency of drying apple core and somehow comfort me. I give a huge sigh of relief and lean against the closed door.

"Are you all right? Do you want to sit down? Can I get you some water?" Jeff asks.

I look at him carefully and remember something else. "I know where I saw you before. It was downtown, at the police station. You looked right at me."

He doesn't answer, so I add, "You can tell me the truth. You lied to me."

"I didn't lie," he says. "I've been with the Houston Police Department for two years. I'm twenty-three, but because I look a lot younger than I am, I was put on a special high school assignment with the narcotics squad, and they sent me to the school in your area. Markowitz got worried about you, and I was in a logical position to keep an eye on you, so you became part of my assignment."

"I was just an assignment?"

"Don't look at me like that, Stacy," he says. "I don't want to hurt you."

"Hurt seems to be another part of growing up," I tell him. "One more thing to get used to."

He shakes his head, resting his hands on my shoulders. I like the feel of them. I wish I could tell him so. I wish I knew how.

"There are so many good things about growing up, you can keep your mind on those and climb over the hurts."

"Like falling in love? I think I was beginning to fall in love with you."

"I don't want to be your first love, Stacy."

"You've made that clear. I won't forget. I'm an 'assignment.'"

"Listen to me," he says, and moves nearer. His hands slip from around my shoulders and hold me tightly, pressing my cheek against the base of his throat. "I asked to get taken off the narcotics assignment just so that I could tell you the truth, and I asked because I care about you."

"But you told me—"

"I said I don't want to be your *first* love. I'd like to be the real thing, and I can wait."

My cheek glows from the warmth of his skin through his shirt, and I can hear the steady beat of his heart. I put my arms around him. I'm Stacy McAdams. I'm seventeen. And I'm definitely in the right body!